D1058834

Under
the Banyan Tree

Under the Banyan Tree

TONI DE PALMA

Holiday House / New York

Thanks are due to Teresa Mlawer of Lectorum Publications, Inc.,
for reviewing the Spanish terms in the novel.

1 3 5 7 9 10 8 6 4 2

Library of Congress Cataloging-in-Publication Data

De Palma, Toni.
Under the banyan tree / Toni De Palma.—1st ed.
p.   cm.
Summary: After her mother leaves, fifteen-year-old Irena runs away from home
and hitchhikes to Key West where she tries to make a better life for herself.
ISBN-13: 978-0-8234-1965-4 (hardcover)
[1. Runaways—Fiction. 2. Mothers—Fiction. 3. Homelessness—Fiction.
4. Key West (Fla.)—Fiction.] I. Title.
PZ7.D3839Un   2007
[Fic]—dc22   2006018719

For A.J.
and
in memory of
Grandma Josie,
my little *nonna*

Acknowledgments

Thank you to the faculty and staff of the Vermont College M.F.A. in Writing for Children and Young Adults program, especially Jane Resh Thomas, my fairy godmother.

A group hug goes out to the Voice, especially to Sheri Cooper Sinykin, Denise Davila, and Mary Rattray, who made Glover 301 feel like home.

To my mother for holding down the fort as I made the trek north.

To Tony for pushing me, which was a good thing.

To A.J., who told his preschool teacher his mother was a writer (He also said his father was a monkey!).

And finally, to Regina Griffin, whose brilliance showed me that patience is indeed a virtue.

1

I took what belonged to me, which wasn't much. A clean pair of underwear, twenty-two dollars in tips I'd made working at Crazy Will's, and the bruise on my right arm. There was nothing else I could take or really wanted. The land the trailer sat on belonged to the state of Florida. The trailer belonged to Daddy's employer, Will Everett. The air in the trailer, humid and smelling of beer, belonged to my father. I would've brought my old Raggedy Ann doll if Daddy hadn't gone and lost her on me. That had been eight years ago when we'd first moved to the Everglades.

Pushing the thought out of my mind, I pointed my ten dusty toes forward and stuck out my thumb. When the semi stopped, the sound of its air brakes pierced the stillness of the early morning. An egret nesting in a tree alongside the trail stretched its wings wide before settling itself down to sleep again.

Damn it. I knew I should've walked the extra half mile down the road before sticking my thumb out. I should've considered how any unusual noise that time of morning could wake a man sleeping only a few yards away.

"Where you headed?" the trucker called down through the passenger-side window.

I looked back toward the trailer, half expecting Daddy to come bursting through the door like a racehorse shooting out of its gate. Any minute and he'd be waving the truck away and yanking me back toward the trailer.

But then I remembered the gator powder and how I'd snuck it into Daddy's beer when he wasn't looking. I relaxed a bit.

"Where you headed?" the trucker repeated. His voice matched the engine's deep rumble.

I hadn't expected to be asked anything. I hadn't expected any of this, though I'd imagined it so many times. The details hadn't mattered—only the feeling of freedom once I was finally away from this place.

The trucker smiled. His lips curled up from under a

2

nicotine-stained mustache and I wondered if I should trust him. When I didn't answer, he spoke instead. "I'm headed to the end. That okay?"

I nodded quickly. After all, it had to be okay. At least for now.

The trucker leaned over and opened the passenger-side door. "Hop in," he said.

I'd never ridden in an eighteen-wheeler before, but I'd studied plenty of truckers getting back into their cabs after they'd had a little too much of Will's Rapid Fire moonshine.

"It's all a matter of balance, Irena," Will used to say whenever I would get frustrated. He'd let me ride up front with him in his truck. Will's truck was no semi, but it did sport two pairs of oversized tires. Will had bartered a couple of rattlers for those tires, and on account of them his truck sat almost as high as the roof of our trailer.

"That a girl, Irena. You can do it," I imagined Will saying as I grabbed the door handle and hoisted myself into the cab. Being tall for fifteen didn't hurt any either.

Before I settled into my seat, the trucker released the clutch and the truck rolled forward. I did the thing I'd promised myself I wouldn't do. I looked back. Through the side-view mirror, I watched the trailer shrink to the size of a small silver bullet. As it did, my heart finally stopped its furious pounding.

When we were well on our way the trucker asked, "What's your name?"

"Irena," I said just short of a whisper.

"Come again?" the trucker asked, cocking his ear.

"Irena," I said again, hoping he heard this time so I wouldn't have to repeat myself. Saying my name aloud, filling the cab of the truck with the sound of it, turned what I'd imagined real, more real than I cared to admit.

"What kind of name is Ee-ray-na?" He pronounced my name in a short, sharp way as if each syllable was a rut in the road he needed to drive around.

"It's Spanish," I explained. "My mother was . . . is Puerto Rican." I prayed he wouldn't ask anything else, like where my mother was or did my parents know that I was hitchhiking.

But all he said was, "My name's Gabriel. But everyone calls me Gabe."

He must've noticed me shifting in my seat because he said, "Yeah. Yeah. I know. Just like the archangel. Believe me. I've gotten into plenty of fights over that one. Guys always asking me where my halo is. Here's my halo I tell them." Gabe made a fist with his right hand, steering the rig with his left.

4

Meat hooks. That's what Will would've called fists like that. Fleshy and powerful. Daddy's hands were small but quick, and his hands were one of the things that made him so darn good at wrestling gators.

When Gabe uncurled his hand and went back to steering, something tight inside me uncurled too. It lay flat and smooth and full of possibility. Keep going, don't turn back, I told myself.

"If I make it to Key West ahead of schedule, there's a bonus in it for me," he explained.

"Key West!" I said. For all my family's hustling about, we'd never made it farther south than the Everglades.

"Yeah, I'm gonna make a load of money once this job's through," Gabe said. "And I've got plans for that money. Big plans. Once I get that money, I'm gonna put a down payment on a piece of land that I've had my eye on for a long time."

An oil rig passed on the opposite side of the road. Gabe reached up, his bicep bulging under his sweat-soaked sleeve, and pulled down on the air horn. *Hooo.* The sound settled in my stomach next to last night's dinner. The cab felt hot, and a tiny stream of sweat welled up behind my knee, trickling down my leg. Behind me, over the spot where Gabe took his naps, a sticky strip flapped in the breeze. The strip was yellow, which made it look like it had been dipped in honey. A mess of gnats and flies stuck to the gummy strip, twisting in the air like they were passengers on some grotesque insect carnival ride. Stuck and without hope. Gnats and flies weren't the only ones who found themselves in such predicaments.

We tooled along down the highway, no one getting in our way until a carload of tourists forced Gabe to slow the rig down.

"Go sightseeing on someone else's nickel!" Gabe screamed. His burly voice made me flinch.

"What's Key West like?" I asked, trying to pull Gabe's mood away from the tourists, who were refusing to speed up or pull off to the side to let him pass.

Gabe palmed the steering wheel with one hand as he rested his elbow on the ledge of the driver's-side window. He spat out his chewing tobacco, trading it for a nonfiltered cigarette. "Crazy town. One too many freaks if you ask me," he said. "You've got your drunks and your potheads but the worst are the writers. They're all filled with funny ideas about the world. You know?"

No, I didn't know. In fact, all the ideas I'd once held true about people were about as spoiled now as the chopped meat Will mixed in with the mush for the gators. But for Gabe's sake, and for my sake too, I nodded like I knew exactly what he was talking about.

For the first time, I noticed the small wooden crucifix hanging from Gabe's key ring. Daddy had no use for religion, but Mama and me would go to services whenever the traveling preacher came down from Sarasota. The preacher was one of those men who, no matter what the temperature outside, rained perspiration.

"Anybody who knows about sin has gotta sweat a lot," Daddy always said.

I was sweating now even more than before. The trickle behind my knee had turned into a full-out stream. The heat made it hard to think, and the steady resolve I'd felt that morning was starting to melt away. What if I wasn't doing the right thing in running away after all? What if I was making a mistake I'd end up regretting forever?

Gabe lit up another cigarette. The smoke swirled around him like some ghostly, sick halo.

"You ain't one of those funny weed people are you?" he asked. He was smiling so I smiled back, but I wasn't sure whether or not he was kidding.

The truck hit a bump and the crucifix wagged at me like an accusatory finger. For the rest of the trip, I sat on my hands, speaking only when spoken to and sitting still as a rock. I concentrated on the wheels turning round and round under me. Faster and faster they spun, but not fast enough.

I studied the clock. It had been blinking 12:22 since I'd boarded. Without a watch, I couldn't tell the time, but by the way the cypress were thinning out, I knew the Everglades were slipping away.

In the side mirror, I caught a look at my arm. The bruise had a deep blue center, but the edges were turning a sickly yellow color. I was grateful that Gabe hadn't asked any questions.

"Oh, cripe!" Gabe cussed. Cussing wasn't anything new to me. Back when Daddy and Will still liked each other, they'd have cussing contests.

"You ol' jackbutt!" Will would say.

"You're nothing but a scum satchel!" Daddy would say, taking his turn.

"Frickertt!"

"Cramwind!"

"Sludge bucket!"

And on and on until Mama was called on to choose a winner.

If Mama announced Will the winner of the contest, Daddy moped around for days afterward.

"Come on now, Dwayne." Mama would try to cajole Daddy. But then she'd ruin it by saying, "After all, Will reads a lot more than you do and he just has a better way with words."

I looked out the cab window to see over the line of cars snaked out in front of us. A tree had fallen across the highway, blocking traffic both ways.

Gabe pulled out another cigarette and lit it. "I better not lose my bonus on account of this." The way he said it, mean and dark, was as if he were blaming me for his bad luck. He slammed his fist against the steering wheel and the crucifix swayed from the vibration.

The dashboard thermometer read ninety-eight degrees, but I felt a shiver working up my back. Was this tree proof that I'd been wrong to run? Or was it God's punishment for using the gator powder? The preacher came to mind, all red and sweaty and talking over and over about the devil and eternal damnation. I figured that was that. God would not allow me to pass without punishment. I was a weed, and no matter what I did, I'd never be able to grow any other way. The few seeds of hope I'd held in my hand were blowing away.

I heard a blast of noise in the distance. Was it the police coming to take me away?

Listening more carefully, I heard *vrooooom, vrooooom.*

Those weren't sirens but chain saws. I supposed that somewhere ahead of us, a road crew was getting ready to clear away the tree.

The tree was a spindly, young one. Soon, the cars ahead of us began to move and I stuck my head out the window. One of the crew, lanky as the scarecrow in *The Wizard of Oz,* looked up from his work in time to give me a friendly wave.

The truck picked up speed, and I sat up high. Tucking one sweaty leg under me, I looked straight ahead and dared myself not to miss a thing of this new life.

2

Just beyond Homestead we picked up Route 1, where the parched browns and greens of the Everglades gave way to turquoise blues and heathery pinks and purples. Green-smocked farmhands hunched over in the fields. Their curved backs looked like big humps of lettuce planted in the sandy soil. From my seat in the semi, these views proved how pretty the world could look.

"Want some?" Gabe asked, offering me a biscuit.

The spongy dough tasted greasy but good. When I finished eating, I sucked my fingers to get the last bit of flavor.

"Hungry, huh?" Gabe asked, offering me another biscuit.

"No thanks. I'm okay," I said. Something about the way Gabe looked at me, like he was sizing me up, left me with an uneasy feeling.

Saying no to that biscuit had been a pretty hard thing to do, because now my stomach was growling worse than one of the panthers Will kept caged behind the shop. Of course I'd felt empty lots of times before, but hunger was a whole new kind of emptiness that made me feel hollow all over, not just in my heart.

Gabe took another hunk of biscuit in his mouth and followed that with a drink from his Thermos. The smell rising up from the Thermos was sweet and dark. Pressing my feet to the floor, I tried hard to ignore the grumbling in my stomach. Instead, I concentrated on the engine's vibrations tickling my feet through the thin soles of my sandals.

"God damn!" Gabe shouted. Bits of biscuit flew out of his mouth from the force of his words.

"What? What?" I said, holding on to the handle of my door. I followed Gabe's stare. There they were, three state police cars sitting off to the side of the interstate waving us in. The lights on one of the cars were flashing like it meant business.

I know a story about a girl who ran away from home. . . .
Will's words drifted into my mind like an old dream.

"Tell me what happened to her?" my eight-year-old self asked. I was new to the Everglades and Will was new to me too. Back then everything Will told me was like a hunk of gold. Precious.

"A nice old man picked the girl up," Will explained. "Told her he'd take her anywhere she wanted to go."

Gabe maneuvered the truck over in the direction of the police cars; the lights, even in the brightness of day, blinded my eyes.

"Did the old man take her somewhere?" I asked Will.

"Sure did." Will nodded. "Took her straight to the cemetery."

When I got older I knew that the purpose of Will's story had been to scare me from trying such a thing. But, as Daddy always reminded me, I wasn't the brightest bulb on the shelf, so there I was.

I stared at the cars, terrified, not knowing who to be more scared of, Gabe or the police. Then I thought of Daddy. Had the gator powder worn off sooner than I'd hoped? Had he been the one to sic the police on me?

"What do they want?" I asked Gabe. Two cops remained in their cars, while one, a woman, got out of her vehicle and directed Gabe to stop.

"What do you *think* they want?" Gabe said. "It's a weigh station. The cusses want to make sure I'm not overweight."

"Overweight? What do the police care whether or not you need to lose a couple of pounds?" I asked, feeling both relieved and confused.

Gabe shook his head and sighed. He pulled the truck to a stop and said, "Just get out."

The weigh station, it turned out, had nothing to do with how fat Gabe was but how much the truck and all the stuff Gabe was hauling amounted to.

"Why don't you stand over there, young lady," one of the police officers—a man this time—said to me. I did what I was told and sat on a bench outside a small building that housed a rest room and a couple of vending machines. I considered using the facilities or spending some of my money to buy a candy bar. But what if I came out and Gabe was gone? What would I do then?

While Gabe filled out some paperwork and two of the three cops looked on, the third officer got up in the cab of the truck and drove it forward a few yards. It was then that I noticed the long metallic strip lying on the road. Was that the scale that did the weighing?

My guess was right. Because as soon as the truck

rolled over the metal strip, the woman officer announced, "You're over."

Gabe cussed some more, but this time he was careful to cuss under his breath. The woman wrote something down on her clipboard and tore off a copy for Gabe.

Gabe grabbed the paper and hurried back toward the truck.

"Hey! Don't forget your kid," one of the officers yelled.

Gabe turned around, his eyes squinting at me. For a moment, I was sure he was going to tell the officers that I was a runaway he'd picked up a few miles back.

"I'll make you a deal," I imagined Gabe telling the cops. "You let me pass on this fine and I'll give you some information that's sure to make the three of you heroes."

But to my surprise, Gabe just said, "Irena! Let's go!"

As soon as we pulled out of the weigh station, Gabe crumpled up the paper and chucked it in the backseat. I couldn't help but smile at Gabe's tiny act of rebellion. After all was said and done, maybe he and I were more alike than I'd first recognized.

The rest of the trip was uneventful. The scare with the police had helped me to forget all about my empty stomach. Now I felt hungry for something else, something that I had no clear vision of, but knew in my marrow existed.

A sign announced the Seven Mile Bridge. Just like that, we lurched forward on a long strip of concrete highway that separated the Gulf of Mexico on one side from the Atlantic Ocean on the other. Aside from the road, nothing but water and sky marked the landscape. All that cool blueness filled me like an empty glass.

Gabe eased his foot off the gas pedal and took another swig from his Thermos. The mile marker showed we were only a few miles out of Key West.

"You have anyone in Key West?" Gabe asked.

The question took me by surprise. What did he care if I had anyone waiting for me? He hadn't exactly struck me as the concerned citizen type. Now that Gabe's trip was nearly complete and he was pretty confident that the bonus was his, was he starting to turn his attention toward me?

"I've got an aunt," I blurted out, expecting the weight of my lie to bring the semi to a stop, the same way that lady officer had done back at the weigh station. But Gabe drove on at a steady speed.

"An aunt, huh?"

Was that doubt I heard in Gabe's thick smoker's

voice? The biscuit that had felt so good and comforting now formed a solid lump in my stomach.

Then I remembered something else Will used to say. "Every story's been told and retold. What makes a story really good are the details."

"My aunt owns a motel," I explained to Gabe, filling in the details. "And I'm gonna go work for her."

Gabe didn't say a word to this, and his silence was worrisome. What if his bonus wasn't the only thing Gabe was looking to claim once we got into Key West? That's why he hadn't given me up to those officers back at the weigh station. If he had, he would've looked pretty bad, picking up an underage hitchhiker, a female no less. But if he brought me to the authorities once we got into Key West that would be different. Gabe could say we'd only met for the first time right there in town and I'd tried to catch a ride from him on my way out of town. Then who would be the one at fault?

Once we got into Key West, I decided I'd make a run for it. Taking to foot in the swamp was one thing. If the cottonmouths didn't get you, the painful cuts caused by the sea of saw grass made you wish you'd come up against one of the deadly snakes instead. But from the little I knew about the Keys, a ribbon of asphalt ran through them, making it easy to run. Something I'd proven I could do already.

For a minute, the semi seemed to be slowing down. Gabe eased his foot off the gas. The sweaty vinyl stuck to my thighs, and I shifted uneasily in my seat waiting for what might come next.

"Which one?" Gabe asked.

"Which one what?" I asked, not understanding his question.

"Which motel?"

"Oh! Which motel," I repeated, stalling for time. I patted my pockets as if I was swatting mosquitoes, pretending to look for something. "I forget the name. I have it written down here somewhere."

Gabe drummed his fingers on the steering wheel.

"If you name some places, maybe it'll come to me," I suggested. Scrunching down my brows, I set my face into a serious look.

"How 'bout the Lido? The Coral Cay? There's one over on the west end called Santiago's Retreat. Or the Albacore Isle?"

I made to open my mouth, to pick any one and be done with it, but then Gabe said, "There's that one off of Spring Street. The Banyan Tree, I think it's called."

"That's the one!" I said.

The Banyan Tree sounded right. The first time I'd seen a banyan was in Bascom, a dirt-road town bordering Alabama on the Florida side. Daddy had just moved us there from Mama's mama's house in New Jersey, and I didn't know a soul. When we pulled up to the battered farmhouse Daddy had rented for us, the first thing I noticed was the banyan.

"Look, Mama! That tree is growing upside down!" I'd said.

"Oh, you silly girl." Mama laughed. "That tree is as right side up as you and me."

"What do you mean, Mama?" I leaned my head far over to the side to imagine what that old tree would look like upside down, which was really right side up. Or was it?

"Here, let me show you, baby girl," Mama said, sneaking up from behind me and grabbing me around the waist. Mama flipped me over and around, my long hair brushing the crabgrass. The world spun round and round, but I didn't mind. I laughed in fact, secure in knowing that Mama would never let me go.

When Mama finally did get tired of holding me, we both landed on the grass in a tumble.

"The whole world looks dizzy." I giggled, the blood still rushing to my head. The blue of the sky and the green grass smeared together like the messy paint pots in my old kindergarten class.

"Oh, you'll get used to it," Daddy said as he walked by carrying some boxes into our new-old house. "Life don't ever seem to straighten itself out no matter how you try to look at it."

After that, Mama and Daddy shared a strange look.

"Banyans are superstrong trees," I told Gabe, more out of nervousness than for any other reason.

"That so?" Gabe said, though I wondered if he really cared a lick about trees or anything else besides money.

"Sure are," I continued because it was better than just sitting there wondering what my next step might be. "Banyans hold up in all kinds of storms, even hurricanes. All those extra roots they grow are like ropes, holding on for dear life." Though it was my mouth that was running a mile a minute, it was Mama's voice I was hearing in my head.

"Don't listen to your father, Irena," Mama had said after Daddy had gone into the house. "This old tree has seen a lot of life and it's still standing strong." And then Mama had done the most marvelous thing. She kissed the tree!

"Mama's in love with the banyan! Mama's in love with the banyan!" I'd chanted, though I wasn't jealous since I knew in my heart that Mama loved me best in the world.

"So the Banyan it is," Gabe said, pressing his foot down hard on the pedal, steamrolling us across the last bridge into Key West.

3

Gabe dropped me off in front of the Banyan Tree.

"See you around, kid," Gabe said and then took off quick to make his delivery.

I was relieved to see him go, glad to have my own two legs under me, instead of eighteen wheels steering my course.

Whoever had named the motel must've been joking or just downright drunk. The peeling clapboard sides and sagging front porch made the place look more like a flophouse than a guesthouse, and not a banyan in sight. Pieces of molding, like drippy icing on a sagging cake and never quite matching, started and stopped all along the roofline. It looked as though someone had tried fixing up the place but never quite finished the job.

I stood in the middle of the sidewalk considering my choices. When Will gave swamp buggy tours, he always pointed out the marker trees. The Seminoles used the young trees, coaxing the branches this way and that, to point to burial grounds and other important places they didn't want their ancestors to forget. If only I had a marker tree, or at least some well-meaning ancestor, to point me in the right direction.

I gave the Banyan one last look-over. It was a sad old place. All the other houses along Spring Street had clipped shrubs and freshened-up paint. The Banyan stuck out like an ugly boil on a pretty girl's face.

Looking down Spring Street, I saw where it merged with another, larger street. Gabe had said that Duval was the main drag in Key West. Maybe this was it!

I headed toward the traffic. Spring Street ran into the main street the way a peaceful stream trickles into a raging river. Teeming with noisy tourists sitting at open-air bars, laughing and talking, the street did indeed turn out to be Duval.

Except for the occasional busload of tourists that came to see the gator shows, I wasn't used to being in the middle of such a crowd. At first, the sights and sounds of Duval—the bright tie-dyed T-shirts flapping outside storefronts, the tinny sound of steel drums, and the heady scent of incense drifting out from curtained windows—were exciting. All those people smiling and having a good time made me feel like I was in the middle of a great big party. But after wandering around awhile with no place to go, all that clinking of glasses and cheerfulness made me tired and dizzy.

The bottoms of my feet burned from all the walking I was doing, and I didn't even have to look to know that a blister the size of a walnut was blooming on my right heel. Why had I chosen to wear sandals? But planning, I was quickly finding out, was not my strong suit.

A heavenly scent of cinnamon and chocolate caught my attention. A shop that sold nothing but sodas and chocolate chip cookies the size of my face was the source of the wonderful smell.

I hadn't meant to wander in, just as I hadn't meant to order a cookie when the guy said, "What can I get you?"

Finding a church with a courtyard away from the rest of the street, I toppled down on the lawn and de-voured my cookie. Just like that and the cookie was gone. Now what? Rather than feeling satisfied, I felt sick. It wasn't just the huge amount of chocolate that had upset my insides, but the realization that I was five dollars lighter and still without a place to go.

My body ached as if I'd carried the eighteen-wheeler to Key West instead of it carrying me. Leaving my old life behind had absorbed every last bit of energy I had, and I snuggled down behind a patch of bushes out of sight from anyone passing by.

How I was capable of dreaming, I'll never know.

"What you doin', Mama?" my dream self asked.

"Planting a garden," Mama said. "Pomegranates and plums and pretty, pretty petunias." She giggled. Even as I slept, I could feel my lips curling up into a smile.

"Mama, you are a pretty, pretty petunia," I said. I buried my face into her smock dress, the cloth feeling like velvet against my cheek.

"Come help me, Dwayne," Mama called to Daddy. "And bring the shovel. I can't seem to lift this rock."

But Daddy didn't come to help. In fact, in my dream Daddy was nowhere to be found.

"I'm askin' your help, Dwayne! Please!" The growing desperation in Mama's voice made me feel antsy, like I had to pee and might not make it to the bathroom in time.

"I've got a shovel!" I said and from out of nowhere, I

produced a shovel. Only the shovel I now held in my hand was red and plastic and better suited to building sand castles, not for digging up big rocks.

"See! I'm getting it. I'll move this rock out of the way for you, Mama!" But the rock wasn't budging, and the longer I kept at it, the more Mama wrung her hands. She wrung her hands so hard, the skin was becoming raw.

"Help me, Dwayne! Help me, why don't you?" The louder Mama yelled, the faster I dug.

When I woke up, the sweet taste of chocolate had turned salty from my tears. I hated that my mind could conjure up such things when I was too tired to have any choice in the matter. And though I hated to admit it, I hated Mama for still having the power she did over me.

Hate. Love. Love. Hate. The two feelings seesawed in my mind up and down, up and down, keeping me off balance.

Mama was gone, had been for six months, and there was no way she was coming back. Both Daddy and Will had made sure of that. But the dream pestered me like a splinter.

I did the only thing I could. I walked. Walking wasn't so bad until I realized I had no place in particular to walk to. Then walking became a trial. As I walked, I noted every street name as if I'd been put in charge of mapping out the city. Key West was a lot bigger than the Everglades with its one highway and acres of swamp. Key West's streets ran into alleys, which turned into foot paths, which sometimes turned into dead ends. If you weren't careful, you could lose yourself for days and, at least in my case, no one would care and come looking for you.

On the waterfront, a boardwalk overlooked the point where the Gulf of Mexico and the Atlantic Ocean meet. Some people were bunched up in a group, looking happy, as if they were waiting for a parade to start.

As I inched up closer, a lady, a little bit older than Mama, smiled at me. Something about her lips, pink, glossy, and inviting, drew me closer.

Rip. The woman tore open a big bag of potato chips and offered the bag to me.

"Take some and pass it around," she said, including me in the group.

Dipping my hand into the bag, I took a handful before reluctantly handing the bag to a little boy to my right. My mouth was parched and the salt stung my lips, but the chips' crunch comforted me. I edged in closer to the lady and the little boy, who looked at me while he chewed his chips. What if the lady was my mother, the little boy my brother? A normal family winding down after a long afternoon of picnicking.

As the sun began to set, everyone watched the horizon. The sun hung low and orange.

On a warm summer night, Mama and Daddy used to put me to bed and then go sit on the front step of our trailer. But sometimes, when I couldn't sleep, I'd sit at the foot of my window and eavesdrop on their conversations.

One night, while Daddy stood with his back flat against the aluminum slats, balancing himself on one leg, the other leg bent up just so, Mama said, "You look just like the Marlboro man, Dwayne."

Mama was puffing away on her cigarette, the smoke drifting in through the same ripped screen I was pressing my nose against, and she sounded happy.

"Oh? Is that so?" Daddy said. He sounded happy too and a little bit coy, like those romantic actors you see on TV who are always trying to make time with the ladies.

"Yeah, that's so. A real cowboy on the open trail." Mama laughed.

I could tell by the way Daddy laughed that he liked what Mama was saying. For me too my parents' sweet talk sounded prettier than all those fancy operas rich people favored so much, especially compared to the way they usually talked to each other.

Then the tide turned. Mama said something I didn't quite catch, and Daddy started cussing.

"You ain't ever happy, Lil," Daddy said. "Always nagging me about something!"

"Well, I'm getting good and fed up with you too," Mama said. At that, she started walking away from Daddy.

"Where you going?" Daddy said, jerking Mama by the arm. Mama dropped her cigarette, but in the dark, the flame-tipped end was still visible.

As my mother walked off into the darkness, I remembered Will's warning when we'd first moved to the Everglades.

"Don't go wandering off in the middle of the night," he'd told me. "You ain't nothing more than something's next meal if you go off out there by yourself."

Terrified at the thought of my precious mother out there in the dark surrounded by gators and snakes, I screamed, "Mama!"

"Get your butt back to bed, Irena!" Daddy screamed back at me.

When it came to Daddy, I had no choice but to

listen. I finally fell asleep close to dawn when I heard the screen door on our trailer rattle shut and Mama say, "It's just me, Dwayne."

If Daddy said anything back, I couldn't hear him. Not over the loud thumping of my own heart that was beating out the words, *Thank you, Jesus. Thank you.*

As the sun set completely, the air turned chilly. And right before my eyes, the sun was swallowed up into the Gulf.

When I looked back, the pink-lipped woman was already gone. The little boy, his fat fist thrust in his mouth, was safely asleep on his father's lap. Along with the sun, my fantasy of a family fizzled into nothing. The only thing hugging me close was my own fear and loneliness.

Now what? When I'd run away, I thought that the loneliness would disappear, but out here without so much as our old dinged-up trailer to anchor me, the world felt even more threatening.

In the center of town I found a little park with a public toilet. Besides needing somewhere to go, I figured it wasn't a bad idea to use the facilities, not knowing the next time I'd have the opportunity. Lucky for me, no one else was in the little cinder block building that housed two bathroom stalls. Using the hand soap from the sink pump, I washed up too, going as far as changing into a clean pair of underwear. But then I realized I had nothing to dry myself with nor anywhere to hang my panties to dry. So I squeezed my underwear out and balled them up in my pocket where they made a wet spot on my shorts. The rest of me—face, hands, and arms—still dripped.

The potato chips had only teased my stomach and hunger pinched at my insides again. Back home, I'd sooner skip a meal than have to sit at the same table with Daddy.

"What's the matter with you, girl?" Daddy said a few days after Mama left us. "Your mama might be gone but that doesn't mean you and me are a couple of animals. You eat at my table when I tell you to."

The last meal we'd eaten together, before I'd broken away, had been a pork hash supper that Daddy had spooned out of the can without bothering to heat it.

"Your mother thinks we can't survive without her," Daddy said. "But we'll show her."

Since when had Daddy and I become a *we*? Sure, Mama had left me too, but no matter what Daddy said or did, I'd never slip over to his side like some kind of traitor. No matter what, it would always be Mama and me.

I remembered how Daddy had shoved the plate of hash at me with such force that, if I hadn't put my hand out in time, the dish would've surely slid right off the table.

"It's good, ain't it?" he'd asked me. As he chewed, the thick stubble on his sunken cheeks pushed out and in, the prickles reminding me of a sea urchin. At the time, the hash, my father, were sickening. But what I wouldn't do now for a plate of that cold, gloppy mess.

On the way into town, I'd noticed a McDonald's. Having blown a good portion of my money already, I needed to budget what was left. Two dollars would buy a cheeseburger and small fries. Mama always said roughage was a good thing to have in your diet, but I passed on the salad. She'd failed to mention that healthier food cost more.

After dinner, I returned to the park, where I used my finger as a toothbrush. I'd passed plenty of hotels and motels in Key West. Big and small ones with nice soft beds, many of which I was certain would go unused tonight. Perfectly good beds with white cotton sheets and chocolates placed on each pillow the way you see them in the movies.

Returning to the church where I'd napped that afternoon, I settled down into a spot between the bushes. There, where the sun had no occasion to fall, the earth smelled sweet and damp and the coarse grass poked at my arms and my legs. In that moment, if someone had had the notion to part the bushes, oh what a fright! For there, coiled like a rattler, I'd be lying. But frightened as they'd be at the discovery of me, their fear would be no match for my own.

4

The hunger was unbearable. It crept out from my belly, reaching into my limbs until my whole body felt hollow. A week had gone by, and my money had run out. How I was going to eat, I didn't know, and not knowing made me ache even worse. Walking was the only thing left for me to do. One step, then another and another. If I moved forward, the mean grumble in my belly didn't seem as bad.

But one day, after I'd counted three missed meals like they were beads on an abacus, I collapsed on someone's front lawn. As I sat down, starved and exhausted, I saw that, across the street, there was an elementary school.

Brrring . . . the school bell rang and a bunch of little

kids—third or fourth graders, I imagined from their size—poured out the back door. Some carried paper bags, others plastic lunch boxes. As the children sat at picnic tables spreading their lunches in front of them, tears burned in my eyes. Life was cruel. Of all the places for me to stop! Someone was rubbing my mistake in my face, only I didn't know who.

I could've picked myself up, ignoring the chirpy little kids who swung their still-short legs as they nibbled happily. But this torture seemed an easier prospect than moving my body somewhere else.

After fifteen minutes, a lunch aide blew her whistle. The children scurried like a colony of ants. Only it wasn't a bit of apple or a breadcrumb that caused the frenzy. It was recess!

Even though I stood a fair distance away, I could see the garbage can filling up quickly with all those half-eaten lunches. When the children, followed by the aides, ran toward a field that was on the opposite side of the school, I saw my way clear and crossed the street.

Still on the sidewalk outside the school yard, I studied the school and the picnic area. The school was a fair distance from where the picnic tables sat, and the garbage can was positioned by an old tree, which hid it from view for the most part.

As I made my way closer to the can, I looked at the school. Was anyone watching me? Would they yell at me if they saw me? Or worse. Would they pity me? The thought of someone feeling sorry for me made me angry, but then my stomach tightened again and I felt dizzy. As much as I hated to admit it, I had no other choice.

A few bees were already swarming around the garbage. Shooing them away, I quickly grabbed three paper bags from the top of the pile and turned back toward the street. Instead of walking, this time I ran. If someone had seen me, they would've thought that I'd just stolen a load of diamonds from a jewelry store, instead of the half-chewed lunches I clutched.

Just down the road I found a dilapidated old house. The mailbox on the porch hung lopsided by one nail and the door was boarded up. Was it abandoned? Curtains hung in the windows, but the windows were caked with grime. I noticed the house had a porch. Glancing from side to side to make sure no one was looking, I stole up the front steps and sat on the floor of the porch.

Digging into the first brown bag, I discovered half of a peanut-butter-and-jelly sandwich. The raspberry jelly tickled my taste buds and the little seeds from the berries snagged in my teeth. The sweetness of the jelly roused my stomach and it grumbled, demanding more.

The second bag held a quarter of a Swiss cheese sandwich, a handful of Cheez Doodles, and the core of an apple. I ate all of it, including the apple core. The third bag held something unrecognizable, some kind of white creamy stuff spread on a piece of celery. The creamy stuff smelled faintly of onions. No wonder the kid had tossed it. Beggars can't be choosers though, so I downed the stuff, holding my breath as I did.

Though it was not a lot, the food had been enough to satisfy me for the time being. I remained on the shaded porch for a while, relaxing in the coolness it provided. The floor was littered with dirt and leaves, and I drew pictures in the grime with my fingers. Though I was probably much too old for things like this, I drew flowers and hearts and arrows piercing those hearts.

"Any cute boys at school?" Mama used to ask when I'd come home from school. Of course that's when I was still going to school, before Daddy's moving us to the Everglades had made that too difficult.

"A couple," I used to tell Mama, mainly because I knew she liked to hear about that sort of stuff. While boys were fine to play dodgeball with, back then I didn't like them in the way Mama meant.

"You've got to pick a good one," Mama used to say. "Boys are like apples. If you choose one with a worm in it, you'll have a life of bellyaches."

Without saying his name, I knew Mama was talking about Daddy. In fact, whenever Mama talked about Daddy, the disappointment in her voice was undeniable.

"Hey! You!" A crabby voice startled me from my daydreams. "Yeah! You! What you doing sitting on old man Flannigan's porch?"

I couldn't tell where the voice was coming from, but I didn't need to sit around and wait to figure it out. I skedaddled right off that porch and didn't look back.

I headed again in the direction of the school. This time, as I skirted the grounds, I could see a group of kids—these a little older than the first group—playing some kind of game. A young male teacher was in charge. He wore sweatpants and a whistle around his neck, similar to the ones the lunch ladies wore. The teacher's golden hair and handsome face made him look like an angel sent from heaven to do good deeds.

Tweeet. When the teacher blew his whistle, the children fell into two orderly lines. One line of kids held hands and faced the other group of kids, who were also holding hands. When the teacher tossed the ball, I recognized the game as one I'd played myself a long time ago.

"Get it!" one boy yelled, and the kids on that boy's team moved forward together in a long, snaky line.

Looking at those kids, seeing how well they worked together, triggered something inside of me. Mama and I had always had that kind of connection. One of us would say go and the other would follow, knowing just what to do. Of course, Daddy was never part of our team. Growing up, I'd always known that by the way he kept to himself. This was something I got used to over the years, but didn't really mind since Mama and I had always been fine together. Better than fine.

Now that was all over. Mama was gone and the connection between us cut. Daddy had made sure of that with what he'd done. That's why I'd used the gator powder.

Sometimes I felt guilty about using the powder, but other times, like now, I felt Daddy deserved it for pushing Mama away from me.

"Now remember, not too much. We still want them to have a little fight left in them," Will had told me the first time I'd seen him use the powder. I watched as he mixed the white stuff into the gators' food. "This is good stuff. I got the recipe off an old Indian."

As Will threw out the food, the gators swarmed around him. Tails flailing, jaws snapping. Will didn't so much as jump. For good reason too. When the gators were eating, they had no interest in biting Will or anyone else for that matter.

"It's the powder," Will said. "They crave it and then it settles them down."

And the gators didn't seem to taste the difference. But when it came to Daddy, I wasn't taking any chances.

"Irena, get me a beer," Daddy yelled one night. He was sitting in his La-Z-Boy watching an old Dirty Harry movie.

"Irena!" Daddy bellowed when I didn't answer fast enough.

"Yes, sir," I said.

Six beers sat in the refrigerator. Six chances to get it right.

When I handed Daddy his beer, it was like a close-up in a movie and I was watching someone else's hand reaching out to give it to him. Half the amount. I'd been careful to cut down the dosage Will normally used on the gators.

"What are you up to?" Daddy said when he saw me looking at him as he gulped down his beer.

"Nothin', Daddy."

He cocked one eye at me, belched out some foul-smelling breath, and said, "Your mother's given me a lifetime of trouble, Irena. I don't need trouble from you too. You hear?"

"Yes, Daddy," I said.

Of course I couldn't just sit there and watch him drink, so instead I sat on the cinder block steps of our trailer and waited. As the sky darkened and the hawks morphed into thin silhouettes against a blazing red sunset, I waited for Daddy to sleep and my world to change.

My stomach churned, only this time it wasn't from hunger so much as it was from a sick, queasy feeling that was building up in the pit of my belly. The queasy feeling quickly changed to sharp, stabbing pains that made it hard to stand upright. Was this my punishment for what I'd done to Daddy?

In one week, the bushes behind the church had become a sort of home for me, a place to rest my head. I'd just about made it back to them before I began throwing up. When I was done puking, I felt worn out and my head seemed like it was filled with an ocean of wiggling, squirming minnows. If it hadn't been for the grace of God and the thought of lying there in a pool of leftover lunches, I would have collapsed onto the ground. Somehow, I managed to get myself out of there.

What a sight I must have been, hair mashed down

against my face, clothes stinking and splattered. Not one person approached me or stopped to ask if I was okay. Hey, this was Key West! The only thing anyone seemed to care about was having a good time. Fine by me. I was getting used to being on my own; didn't want their help anyway. How many times had Will told me I was too thin-skinned? This was good. A test. If I could get through this, everything would turn out okay.

Back at the park, I jiggled the knob on the bathroom door. It was shut tight for the night. Who would lock a public toilet!

My mind was a jumble of ideas and feelings. Maybe running away had been a stupid idea. At least with Daddy, I always knew what to expect.

The park was nearly empty, except for a few stragglers. The lights hummed, and the scent of oleander hung in the air. The smell reminded me of the perfume some of the old ladies who came to see the gator show doused themselves with, and for a minute I thought maybe I'd dreamed the past week.

"Hey, kid! Need some help?" The voice came from a bench to the right of the building housing the bathroom. The bench was hidden behind some oleander bushes and that's probably why I'd never noticed it before.

I poked my head around the bushes to see who had

spoken. The person I found looked like a kid—about my height and age—but there was something about his sloping shoulders and long face that made him look like a man.

"What are you staring at?" he asked.

Dropping my eyes to the ground, I shrugged and said, "Nothin'."

We stood there, him and me, not saying a word. But then, I caught a glimpse of a bag by the bench. Inside the bag, I saw a rolled-up blanket and a tattered paperback book. An old rag teddy bear was shoved in the bag too, head down with its tattered legs sticking up. I couldn't help but think of my own Raggedy Ann doll. The kid was a street person.

"Need some help?" he asked.

His question startled me. *He* wanted to help *me*? But then again, I was homeless too.

I nodded but when I stepped too close behind him, he shot me a look and I stepped away, giving him some space. Over his shoulder, I watched what the kid was doing. He'd pulled a thin metal rod from out of his pocket. It looked like a knitting needle cut down to the size of a pencil stub. Inserting the rod into the bathroom lock, he wiggled it a bit until there was a click.

"It's all yours," he said, backing away to let me by. For

the first time, I noticed how flimsy and thin his clothes were and how his wrists jutted out from his sleeves like two meatless drumsticks. How long had *he* been living on the streets?

He threw me the metal rod and said, "Good luck!" Then he walked away.

Inside the bathroom, I clicked the lock in place. It was the kind of public bathroom with one sink and two stalls and not much else. After washing my face and rinsing out my mouth, I cleaned the vomit off my shirt. A few swallows of cool water tasted wonderful and settled my mind as well as my stomach.

I took the metal rod from my pocket. What was the kid's name? Where was he from? I would've liked for him to stick around. But then I remembered the look in his eyes, like Will's panthers—cagey and frightened.

What had the kid said when he'd handed me the metal rod? Good luck? I pressed it into the palm of my hand. Like a key, that's how he'd used it.

That night, I slept on the bathroom floor. The tile was cold and hard and I tried not to think about the unimaginable muck living and growing next to me. All night long, I held on to my key. For that's how I'd come to think of it. A scrap of junk that could open doors.

5

A slice of sunlight slipped through the vent above the door. A brand-new day. Determined to start off on the right foot, I washed my face, ears, and hands. The extra pair of underwear I'd shoved into my pocket was only slightly damp now. I changed and washed out my other pair. My reflection in the mirror showed the way my hair snagged at the crown. The night before, I'd washed it out in the bathroom sink, raking the tangles with my fingers. The vomit splotch had faded and blended in with the rest of the swirly design on my T-shirt, but it was my eyes that startled me.

"You have what they call cat's eyes," Mama once told

me. "Your grandmother had them too. A lot of people find eyes like yours a little hard to look at," Mama explained. "On account of most people don't really want to be seen."

"What do you mean, Mama?" I'd asked her each time she called me her little cat-eyed girl. "Why don't people want to be seen?"

"Oh, people want to be seen on the outside for sure. They want to show off their fancy cars and houses and expensive jewelry. But most people don't want anyone to see what's on the inside, the stuff that's bubbling up just out of view."

Looking at my eyes in the mirror now, all I saw were a pair of dark, smudgy circles, like crescent moons, tattooing the skin under my eyes. All those times Mama had explained and I still didn't understand. My eyes might have had an unusual shape, like flat almonds, but I knew nothing about what made people do what they did, not even my own mama.

Bowing my head, I turned my attention back to my fingernails. Running the water to full-steam hot, I soaked my fingers until they turned red.

Sneakers thudded on grass in the park outside. I couldn't stay in the bathroom all day. Sooner or later, someone would feel the urge, and if they saw me lurking around they might report me to the cops.

Touching my pocket, I made sure my lucky charm was safe. That night, when everyone cleared out of the park and the bathroom was locked up for the night, at least I'd have a place to stay.

Back on the streets of Key West, I walked along Whitehead Street. A little boy fidgeted in front of a sign tacked to a high brick wall. The sign said, THE ERNEST HEMINGWAY HOME AND MUSEUM. The boy's father paid the entrance fee and he and the boy disappeared behind the wall. Other people followed and I stood on tiptoe trying to get a peek. Whoever Ernest Hemingway was, he'd managed to build the wall high enough to keep people like me out.

I headed for the boardwalk. Waiters dressed in crisp white shirts and black slacks dashed about serving breakfast to customers sitting lazily at outdoor cafes. The smell of fresh-brewed coffee mingled with the salt air, and my stomach reminded me that it would not be ignored much longer.

Willing myself away from the delicious smells, I walked along the water instead. White sailboats skimmed along the surface in teams of four and six, while gulls looped and dove. One gull dipped his beak into the surf, effortlessly pulling out a squirming fish. The bird, breakfast in mouth, flew a direct path south. A mixture of stupidity and jealousy welled up inside of me. How could a common old gull manage better than me?

When I had had money and could still afford a burger at McDonald's, I noticed that most of the counter help were teenagers no older than me. A sign said: HEY KIDS! APPLY NOW! GREAT BENEFITS AND FREE MEALS DURING YOUR SHIFT.

Taking a deep breath, I marched up to the only adult working the counter.

"May I help you?" he asked.

Service with a smile. I liked that, thought it held promise.

"I'd like to fill out an application," I said.

The man handed me a form and a pen. I sat at a table to fill out the form, the smell of oily french fries squeezing my insides. As soon as I handed the application in, I would ask the man to let me start right away.

"How's it coming along?" the man asked. He looked at the form and frowned. I was sure he was noticing all the places I'd left blank.

I pushed my hand in my pocket and pressed the little metal bar for good luck.

The man thumped his pointer finger on his chin. "You forgot to put down your social security number," he said.

"Lost my card," I said. It wasn't really a lie. So much of me was lost, had been lost; my doll, my home, my mother. In the scheme of things, what were a few lost numbers?

"Come with me," the man said.

I followed him behind the counter to the kitchen, where the burgers were assembled. A boy my age layered onions, pickle, tomato, lettuce, and ketchup onto a beef patty before topping it off with a soft brown bun. Just watching him made my stomach turn over like a dog performing tricks.

I could do that. I knew I could. I could memorize the exact order, in synchronized sequence. I could be the best hamburger maker in the world if I could eat one every now and then.

I was about to tell the man this, sing the McDonald's pledge of allegiance if that's what it took. Anything, just to get a job, some food, a place.

Before I could work up the nerve, the man said, "Hey, Rudy, toss me over one of those burgers."

The boy handed the man a double cheese. The man put the burger in a bag along with a large fries and a Coke. Then, he handed me the bag.

I looked inside, noticing how everything was perfectly nested so the fries didn't spill and the burger didn't roll out of its wrapper. Okay, so rookies didn't get to handle the meat right off. I needed to learn how to bag the goodies first, respect the food, before being allowed to touch it.

But then the guy said, "Go ahead. Take it."

I took the bag not understanding. Was this part of the training? Did he expect me to pull his work apart, make it better?

"Go ahead. Take it," he repeated. And then I understood why. When I looked at him, his eyes held a steady gaze on the floor.

Without those numbers on my application, I didn't exist. Without those numbers, I couldn't have the job.

The fryer spat grease, and Rudy stood there staring at me. His mouth hung open like a hook had caught in it. Angry red pimples like tiny fire ants pebbled his cheeks. He didn't look like the brightest kid in the world, but between me and him, it was obvious who had the upper hand here.

With my pride feeling shriveled up worse than one of Rudy's overcooked patties, I took the bag. Words rose inside of me like stinging bile, but I couldn't speak them. All I could do was nod my thanks to the man.

As I was leaving, the man said something about coming back . . . *when you find those numbers.*

Find numbers. Unlock doors. Come back. The words set my rhythm. Only this time, I wasn't walking. I was running.

6

The turning point came that night. While I waited for the park to clear out, I entertained myself by peeling off the flaking specks of green paint dotting my bench. The clock on the old cigar factory chimed nine o'clock and a young man with greasy hair sat on the ground strumming the same chord on his guitar. The music sounded soft and mellow, and the musician sang the same word, *whippoorwill, whippoorwill,* over and over again. Like everything else in my life, the song made no sense.

When the rain started, I half had the notion that the warm wetness slipping down my cheeks might be tears, but I was wrong. The rain started off slowly but then the trickle changed into bucketfuls of water that splashed up hard. Everyone scrambled out of the park. Even the musician, so lost in his music, grabbed his guitar and made a beeline for Duval Street. From living in the Everglades, I was used to storms like these, great washes of water passing over the land as quickly as they came. In the past, I'd always had shelter, a way to defend myself against those pelting blasts of water.

I ran for the bathroom and turned the knob. Locked. Inserting the metal rod into the lock, I prayed. Fumbling, I imagined there was a notch or some small depression the rod needed to slip into. How had he done it, and why hadn't I paid closer attention?

Only a slight twist of my wrist and there it was. A minor adjustment, a small change in gesture had made a difference and, *click!* The lock released and I entered the bathroom. Flipping on the light, I took a quick look under the stalls. No feet, but what did I expect? Another runaway like me? I turned the lock from the inside of the bathroom, locking myself in and anyone else out.

The bathroom had seemed like such a haven the night before. Now it was more like a prison. The humidity intensified the smell of urine. The toilet seat, pockmarked with cigarette burns, was filthy and the sink was littered with strands of hair, none of which matched my own.

Covering my ears, I was able to push out the deafening noise coming from the steady rain clattering down on the bathroom's tin roof. But the sound of my own thoughts seeped in.

Stupid! Stupid! What had I expected? What had I ever expected?

"High hopes are a sure formula for disappointment," Mama always said. But I'd assumed she was talking about Daddy.

The tears came. Hot, self-pitying, wasted tears. I hugged my legs, pulling them into my chest, pushing out my breath in deep, gut-wrenching heaves.

When the rain finally stopped, the bathroom was silent. I felt tired and hungry and something else. Cold. Surprisingly cold. This was Key West in the springtime and I was teeth-chattering cold. With my head on my knees and my arms folded to form a makeshift pillow, I fell asleep sitting up on the floor.

The night Mama left for good, I learned a new style of sleeping. I resisted sleep's deeper pull on my body and settled instead for a sort of half slumber. In this state of half sleep I heard someone rustling around outside. A hint of dull light slipped through the air vent above the door and I sensed the morning must still be very new. The doorknob shook and my spine tingled as if someone had trailed a feather up and down my back. The doorknob rattled again, the silver metal ring around the base of the knob shaking loosely like a bracelet on an angry woman's wrist.

I held myself tighter, waiting. But when the doorknob stilled and there was only silence, I did not feel relief. Instead, a swell of sadness rose up from my belly, suffocated me, pulled me down. I was drowning. Something about that rustling noise, how it was there one moment but slipped away the next, touched off a memory I'd not wanted to think about for a long time.

The first slipping away had happened shortly after we'd come to live in the trailer parked next to Crazy Will's gator show.

Mama breezed into my room one morning. "Daddy's taking us out for the day, Irena!" she said. She then attacked the big pile of laundry that had been sitting in the corner of my room for the last two months. The thought of getting away from the Everglades—even if it was only for a day—had infused Mama with a new energy, enough to tackle the long-forgotten laundry. Her hands worked swiftly, smoothing out wrinkles in white T-shirts, underwear, and a polka-dot skirt I'd long outgrown.

"We're going in Will's truck?" I asked, climbing in between Mama and Daddy, who was already sitting behind the steering wheel.

"Our old truck won't get us anywhere we want to go," Mama said. "So Will was nice enough to loan us his."

Next to me, I felt Daddy's back stiffen. I'd noticed that lately, any time Mama mentioned Will's name, Daddy looked like someone had stuck him with a hot poker.

But this time, Daddy didn't just sit there silently burning up on the inside. This time, a puff of smoke came out of him, a sign of the full-out inferno that would blaze up later on.

"Well, if Will paid me what I was worth I could fix my own truck," Daddy said to Mama.

"Ha! What you're worth?" Mama said.

Daddy's fist balled up in his lap, but I heard him take a breath and the fingers uncurled one by one. Sitting between the two of them, I felt like a piece of salt water taffy being pulled in opposite directions. The whole rest of the ride was passed in uncomfortable silence.

"This is your idea of a day out?" Mama whined

when she caught sight of the billboard advertising the dog races.

Ignoring Mama's comment, Daddy spat out the window and steered into the parking lot. He paid the parking lot attendant the two-dollar parking fee and an extra dollar so we could park close to the gate.

After we found our seats, Daddy asked, "You want to go check out the dogs?"

Mama sat in her seat, her arms folded over her chest, and she stared straight ahead, ignoring Daddy.

"What about you, Irena? Want to come see the dogs so as we can pick the best ones to bet on?"

Daddy stood there, his long arms hanging loosely at his sides. Just below the sleeve of Daddy's undershirt was a red scar where he'd gotten nipped by a gator. Back then he was still trying, and I had to give credit where credit was due.

"Okay," I said, looking at Mama, who didn't so much as flinch when a fly landed on her hand.

Me choosing Daddy over Mama came as a surprise even to Daddy, who said, "Well. Okay. Yeah. Good, now let's go see the dogs."

We walked out a different gate than the one we'd entered by, and the closer we got to the dogs, the worse the smell got.

"Nothing like the smell of good dog shit," Daddy said.

I tried hard not to breathe and when Daddy wasn't looking I put my hand over my nose. The smell was bad, but the sight of those poor animals locked in cages stacked one on top of the other was a sight that brought tears to my eyes.

"You cryin'?" Daddy asked me when he caught me wiping my eyes with the back of my hand.

"No, Daddy. I just got something in my eye," I said. I lied because I knew that telling Daddy the truth would only disappoint him, and I guess back then I still held a glimmer of hope for me and him.

One particularly sorrowful-looking creature caught my eye. On the front of the cage was a three-by-five card with the dog's name printed on it: Smiley's Rascal.

"I like him, Daddy," I said the way most kids would say they liked a bike or a toy they saw in a store window.

"You do, do you?" Daddy said. "He doesn't look like much to me, but if you want me to put some money down on him, we'll give him a try."

Placing a bet on the skinny little greyhound wasn't what I'd had in mind. Secretly, I'd hoped that Daddy would save the little dog, tell the man who owned him that his little girl had taken a fancy to the dog and we wanted to bring it home to be our pet.

But Daddy was already pulling me away. "Let's go, Irena. The races are about to start," Daddy said. And as we were walking back to our seats, he said to himself more than me, "I sure hope that woman ain't still on the rag."

Daddy went to wager and returned with a big bucket of popcorn and a Coke with a lot of ice. Accepting Daddy's gesture, Mama settled back, grabbing up handfuls of popcorn. As the races began, she pointed out people and made comments about their looks or the way they carried themselves.

"I wouldn't be caught dead wearing that dress," Mama said about one lady a few rows ahead. I didn't think the lady's dress was all that bad and in fact, I found her quite pretty, though I wouldn't admit this to Mama.

Mama chewed her popcorn thoughtfully, and I was happy that she seemed to be enjoying herself.

"There's your dog, Irena," Daddy said, pointing to gate number four. I couldn't see much of the mangy fellow.

At the mention of number four, Mama lit into Daddy. "What's the matter with you Dwayne? Irena's too young to be gambling."

"It's not her money she's gambling with," Daddy said. "She just chose the dumb animal."

A loud clap of noise interrupted Mama and Daddy's argument and the dogs were off. Smiley's Rascal shot out of the gate along with the rest of the pack. My skinny favorite was surprisingly fast. His thin gray snout pointed straight as an arrow as it circled the track, chasing the fake rabbit attached to a mechanical arm that moved around the oblong field. Later on Will would tell me that the reason the dogs ran so fast was because they were starving and the promise of a rabbit dinner was enough to get even the slowest dog going.

Smiley's Rascal bound along in the middle of the pack, making a good effort. Then something happened. One of the front dogs got too close to the inside rail and stumbled. Smiley's Rascal, along with a few other dogs, barreled into the first dog and, in an instant, their twisted bodies were flying in every direction.

The crowd groaned in unison and Mama stopped eating her popcorn.

I cried the whole way home.

"You and your stupid ideas," Mama said. Her words smelled of fake butter. "You've gone and traumatized her for the rest of her life."

"How was I supposed to know they shoot the damn dogs right there on the field?" Daddy said, defending himself.

The truck hit a bump in the road and I flinched, same as when I'd heard them shoot Smiley's Rascal right straight in the head.

That night, I couldn't close my eyes without seeing Smiley's Rascal, his skinny body twitching for a few seconds more right after they'd shot him.

Mama came in to check on me. "Go to bed, Irena," Mama had said. She had parted the curtains on the window to look out and mistakenly let the moon in. It was then that I knew that all of us—me, Daddy, and Mama—were like the moon and all the other planets. We were somehow part of the same universe, but we all had our own paths and someday there was a danger that one of us might slip out of our orbit altogether.

That memory was a turning point. Even though my heart felt heavy, I forced myself up from the bathroom floor, unlocked the door, and got out of there. For some reason, my heart, more than my head, steered me back to the Banyan Tree. Standing outside the motel like I was waiting for something, I had no idea what that something might be. Almost two weeks had passed since Gabe had left me off in this exact spot, but the time felt more like a year. I could poke through the bottom of my left sandal with my big toe, and my clothes were in sore need of laundering. My shorts dragged around my waist on account of the weight I'd lost, but most of all I was dead tired.

I had changed, but the motel looked the same, disheveled and sad. No one went in or came out, but the rest of the street seemed to go about its business in an ordinary way. A man, dressed in shorts and a T-shirt, came out of the house next door.

"Have a nice day," his skinny wife told him before he headed down the street.

A boy with flaming red hair and freckles came out of the house on the other side of the Banyan. He straddled his two-wheeler and rode up and down the sidewalk like some kind of hotshot. Each time he passed me, he inched his bike a little closer in my direction. One time he got so close, I could've sworn I smelled the bacon he'd eaten that morning for breakfast. Even worse were the looks the boy shot me each time he passed, as if I was some lowly worm he was bent on squashing.

Remembering Daddy's posture when he faced a gator, I stood my ground, shoulders back, head held high. The only problem was the ground I was standing on didn't belong to me and this snot-nosed kid knew it.

The kid reached the end of the block. He turned his bike around, ready to take another crack at me, when the door of the Banyan flew open. A woman stood on the porch, her hands steadied on the rail as if she were bracing herself against the wind. And then she screamed.

"Anthony Joseph Plotford! I'm going to tell your mother on you!"

7

The boy, startled at hearing his name bellowed so publicly, bent his head in shame and rode away.

Standing there, absentmindedly poking my toe through my sandal, I probably should've done something. Finally, I willed my legs to move and began to walk away.

"Don't go!" I was surprised. The lady who'd yelled at Anthony Joseph Plotford was now talking to me. "Don't go," she repeated. "You're the young lady who called about the chambermaid job, yes?"

"The what?" I asked.

"The chambermaid job. You *are* looking for a job, aren't you?"

A nervous tickle fluttered in my throat. Well, of course I was looking for a job. If you could call a dying man's search for water just *looking*.

But there was something comfortable about the woman's slouch, the way her bosom peeked over her crossed arms as if she were embracing two puppies, that forced me to tell the truth. "Yes, ma'am. I am looking for a job, but I wasn't the one who called."

"Too bad." The woman tsked.

"I'd like to help you out, ma'am," I told her. After all, she had saved me from a tyrannical ten-year-old. But without a social security number, I didn't even see the point in trying.

The woman waved me closer to her and I stepped forward. She smelled nice. Not perfume nice, but food nice. My stomach lurched.

"I don't understand," the woman said. "You need a job and I have a job. So what is the problem?"

For the first time, I noticed that the woman held a toothpick in her mouth that bobbed when she spoke.

"I don't have the right papers," I said.

"Papers?" she asked. She looked at me from top to toe. "You don't look like a dog to me."

"No," I said. I couldn't help but smile. "You know. A social security number."

"Oh, that!" The woman waved her hand, releasing a delicious smell. I was tempted to bite into the air to get a taste of it.

She introduced herself. "I'm Carlotta."

"I'm Irena," I said, introducing myself back.

"I tell you what, Irena," Carlotta said. "I'm trying out a new recipe. Come in and give me your opinion. We'll see what happens from there."

Will was forever picking up strays along the trail. He'd lure them into his truck with one of the biscuits he kept in the glove compartment.

"He's a true-blue, good-hearted person," Mama used to say.

I followed Carlotta as obediently as one of Will's hungry dogs.

The Banyan was nothing more than an old house, converted into a motel. Two couches the color of the summer sky sat in the living room. I wondered how it might feel to curl up on one of them. An old grandfather clock ticked away the minutes drowsily—*tick, tick, tick*—giving the impression that life in the motel moved at a slower pace.

The living room connected to a dining room, where a girl, a few years older than me and pregnant, sat writing numbers in a ledger.

"Lynette, this is Irena," Carlotta said.

Lynette, her eyes half hidden beneath a fringe of dark black bangs, barely glanced up from her numbers, which ran in long penciled columns that Lynette erased, rewrote, then erased again. Each time she made a correction, she sighed as if the numbers were a group of naughty children that she just couldn't quite manage.

"In here," Carlotta said. She shooed me into the kitchen and pointed to a chair where I should sit.

I glanced around the kitchen. It was old but clean and cheery. On the counter sat a plate heaped with grapes and figs and mangos. Beside the plate were other plates covered with tin foil holding God knows what other glorious things.

"Do you like bread and jam?" Carlotta asked me.

I nodded. Yes, I liked bread and jam or bread and ham or bread and pickled beets for all I cared. I liked any kind of food.

Carlotta poked her head into the dining room and asked Lynette, "Would you like a little snack, *mi hija?*"

Mama had taught me a little Spanish, and I knew that *mi hija* meant "my child." When Carlotta said the words, her voice was sweet as if it had been dredged in sugar.

But Lynette's reply was not sweet. "No!" she sniped

back and though I didn't know her very well, I felt insulted for Carlotta.

Carlotta returned to the counter, obviously not bothered by Lynette, and began slathering jam on pieces of thick bread. Five, six, seven slices. Enough, I supposed, even if Lynette did change her mind.

"That Lynette," Carlotta said. "She worries too much, never takes a minute to eat a little something."

Carlotta set the entire dish in front of me. "I make the best Cuban bread on the Key." The way she said it, so matter-of-fact, I could tell she was not boasting. "My own jam too," Carlotta explained. "I'm always trying to get it perfect."

Carlotta stared at me expectantly so I knew it was okay to take a bite. The combination of the soft bread and the jam woke up my sleeping taste buds. A mixture of apricots, peaches, nuts, and something else I couldn't quite put my finger on exploded inside my mouth.

Reading my face, Carlotta said, "It's cumin. I try to put a little bit of my parents' homeland into everything I cook."

"Where is that?" I asked, eager to hear about anyone's home, even if it wasn't mine.

"I was born in this country," Carlotta explained. "But my parents were born in Cuba. Oh, how Papa wanted to return. But my poor papa went to his grave without ever seeing his homeland again."

Carlotta was also stuck between the old and the new.

"About the job," Carlotta said. "You'll have a room to yourself and your meals. I'm afraid the pay isn't much."

A room and food and pay too! I couldn't believe my luck.

"Are you sure it will be okay?" There was still the issue of the social security number, but more than that, I knew that things didn't just slide into place that easily. There had to be a catch.

Carlotta picked up a slice of bread and spread a layer of jam on it. The toothpick, still in her mouth, bobbed as she chewed.

"All I know," Carlotta said, "is that you appreciate good food, Irena. And you didn't let that Plotford kid get the better of you. That tells me something about you."

I poked around at the bottom of my sandal.

Carlotta lifted the lid off a canister and produced a small plastic bag filled with tiny brown seeds. Cumin, it turned out, was a spice. When Carlotta added it to the jam, it seemed to pull all the other ingredients together, making them come alive in my mouth.

"Too much will make it bitter," Carlotta cautioned.

I watched as the tiny brown slivers settled on the

surface of the bubbling syrup. Slowly, the heat did its work and the cumin was drawn down into the pot, becoming part of the whole wonderful sweet mixture.

Carlotta asked about my family.

"My mother's been gone for a while," I explained.

"You poor thing," Carlotta said. "I remember how difficult it was when my papa died. I was only a few years younger than you."

I was tempted to correct Carlotta, but her compassion felt warm and comforting and I didn't want to let it go.

Daddy was harder to explain. I told Carlotta that Daddy traveled a lot for work and that even when he was home, he preferred his alone time.

"Ah! A contemplative man," Carlotta remarked. "Is he religious?"

"Oh, he's always praying," I said. Jesus, Mary, and Joseph! Daddy always called on the holy family whenever he ran low on beer.

What I told Carlotta weren't lies exactly, just wrinkled stories, which were fine the way they were and didn't need any real straightening out.

"Come, Irena. I'll show you the rest of it," Carlotta said.

"You mean there's more?"

"Oh, you didn't think this was where the guests stayed, did you?"

We walked out the kitchen door that led to the enormous backyard. The grass was thin in some spots, thick and green in others. Did all the other houses along Spring Street hide such large yards? With the house on one side, three rows of whitewashed stucco rooms, topped with orange terra-cotta roof tiles, lined the perimeter of the backyard. The rooms, sixteen in all, formed a large courtyard in the middle. In the center stood an ancient banyan tree—the biggest, most glorious banyan I'd ever seen—draped in delicate garlands of Spanish moss.

And there in my mind stood Mama kissing the banyan.

"Come, Irena. I want to show you something." Carlotta gestured toward the trunk of the tree. "See here," Carlotta said. She pointed to a place on the trunk that was scraped away. "When we were just engaged, my husband, Freddie, carved our initials right there."

I looked carefully at the spot where Carlotta was pointing. The bark there was slightly frayed and a bit lighter than the rest of the trunk, but nothing resembled initials.

"Oh, it's there all right," Carlotta said. "The tree has healed itself, that's all. But our love, it's still there under the skin of the tree." Carlotta patted the tree as if it were the shoulder of a good friend.

In kindergarten, the teacher had taught us that trees were living, breathing things just like people, but I'd never considered that trees could see things or experience life in the same way people did.

The banyan's leaves provided a shady spot for anyone sitting in the courtyard, and a number of folding chairs were scattered around its knotty base.

"We have sixteen rooms in all. Five, including your own, are taken. But that can change from day to day, week to week," Carlotta explained.

She showed me around. Except for the doors, which were painted in a rainbow of colors, the rooms were identical. Each one contained a double bed, a dresser, two lamps, and a clock radio. Each guest had a shower, and, if they chose, they could share meals in the dining room with Carlotta and the rest of the staff.

"When guests come back, they ask to stay in the purple room or the green room," Carlotta explained.

Guests? Besides Lynette, Carlotta, and me, I hadn't seen anybody else.

"And this will be your room. The sunny yellow

room." Carlotta turned the key in the lock of the yellow door, but it stuck.

"This darn lock is always getting jammed." Carlotta huffed as she struggled to unlock the door.

Shoving my hands into my pockets, I touched my good-luck key!

"Can I try?" I asked. I showed Carlotta the finger-length piece of metal I'd used to pick the bathroom lock. She agreed to let me try.

Opening my new door proved easier than opening the one to the bathroom.

"How clever of you, Irena," Carlotta said.

It'd been so long since anyone had complimented me that I felt a hot flush rise along my neck and travel across my cheeks.

I looked back at the banyan and the chairs in its shade. One of them was yellow, like my door. Now I saw. Each room had a chair to match the color of that room's door. Each guest had a chair and a place under the banyan.

Before following Carlotta, I glanced back at the empty chairs. Some leaves had collected on a few of them, but mine was bare. My chair? My room? My spot on Earth? Could it have been here all along, just waiting for me to find it?

A gray tabby cat dozed beneath the banyan. His paws twitched as he chased his dream mouse. The sun streaming through the branches left dappled patterns of sunlight on his coat. I felt a ripple of fear for the poor thing. How would he feel once he woke up to find out it had all been just a dream?

8

Carlotta handed me a ring of keys. Red, turquoise, green. A whole rainbow of keys to unlock a rainbow of doors.

"You can start tomorrow," she said. "And when dinner is ready, I'll call you."

After the door closed behind her, I sat on the edge of my bed, amazed. The room was smaller than the double-wide I'd shared with Mama and Daddy, but it was clean. After Mama left, Daddy said, "Good riddance." And our home quickly became cluttered with newspapers, beer bottles, and any other old trash that Daddy could bring home to fill all the cracks and hollow places left behind by Mama's not being there.

I walked into the bathroom and found a fluffy blue towel hanging from the bar. Tiny soaps, shaped like conch shells, sat in a dish on the sink. Back in my room, a jalousie window, set with water glass, softened the sunlight falling into the room. I cranked the window open and lilac-scented air drifted in. Stretching out on the lace coverlet, my eyelids felt like sacks of sand weighing heavy on my head and I fell asleep.

This time I dreamed we were having a picnic, just Mama and me under the banyan tree. A cold roasted chicken, corn on the cob, and homemade bread-and-butter pickles were spread out on one of Mama's good blankets. As I crunched on a pickle, a great gust of wind swirled around us, lifting Mama and me, along with our whole picnic, into the air.

I grabbed onto one of the banyan's branches and screamed, "Mama! Hold on to the tree!"

Mama couldn't hear or maybe she just didn't care to hear. Another gust of wind blew her right away from me.

My hands tightly gripped the banyan's gnarled limb. Mama couldn't be that far off already. Should I let go too? But if I let go, then what? Holding on meant I'd be safe, but risk losing Mama forever.

Before I could decide what to do, I woke up.

In the bathroom, I took one of the pretty soaps and

scrubbed. By the time I was done, my skin tingled and the soap had melted down to the size of a lentil.

The sound of clattering dishes floated through my window and that simple sound signaled to my stomach to roll over as if it were a happy puppy expecting a treat. But before I headed back to the main house for dinner, I paid a visit to the banyan.

The courtyard was empty, yet I still watched to make sure no one could see me as I ran my hand over the spot Carlotta had showed me. I wondered. If a tree could feel love, might it also grant wishes? Pressing my hand against the rough bark, I made my wish.

"Supper time!" Carlotta called out from the kitchen window.

Carlotta's voice bounced off the walls of the court-yard like a bird's song, and my puppy-dog stomach now turned into a ravenous wolf.

Five place settings were laid out on the knotty wood table in the dining room.

A plump man, a little older than Carlotta, wobbled into the dining room. *"¡Qué mesa tan bonita!"* he exclaimed, looking at the lovely table. The man reminded me of a hound dog with his deep, sagging jowls and large eyes that turned down at the corners, giving him a slightly sad appearance.

Juggling a platter of chicken and rice, Carlotta introduced the man to me. "Antonio, this is Irena. Irena, this is my brother, Antonio."

"*Mucho gusto,*" Antonio said.

"*Mucho gusto,* Don Antonio," I repeated back.

"*¡Ah! ¡Hablas español!*" Don Antonio exclaimed when he thought I spoke Spanish.

"No, no," I tried to explain. "Only a few words here and there."

"Hmmph! Let's hope you're better at cleaning." Lynette snickered as she too waddled into the room. Unlike Don Antonio, who wore his fat all over, Lynette's weight was all in front of her. I imagined how unsteady this made her and how with one tiny push she'd easily topple over.

For my sake, Don Antonio spoke to me now in English. "But your name? It is Spanish, no?"

Carlotta butted in. "Oh! Antonio. Leave the child in peace. She just got here and already you are playing fifty questions!"

"The game is called twenty questions, Carlotta," Don Antonio corrected. "Besides, I am just being friendly. You don't mind, do you, Irena?"

"No," I said, pulling a piece of chicken from the

bone. But with the things I'd already told Carlotta and the suspicious glare Lynette was sending my way, I filled my mouth with food, hoping no one would ask me any more questions.

"Yes. I'd love to hear all about you," Lynette piped in. Will had a name for people who liked to make trouble. Bullet makers, he called them. And that was exactly what Lynette was.

The chicken caught in my throat and I started coughing. Carlotta passed me a glass of water.

"Enough talk! Eat!" Carlotta said, and even Lynette shut up.

Lucky for me too, Don Antonio was more interested in his food than he was in me. He shoveled it into his mouth, setting his jowls into a happy dance with each bite.

Happy for the food and most of the company, I chewed every bite of chicken ten times before swallowing, hoping to make the food and the moment last. I resisted the temptation to lick my plate. I didn't want to admit my hunger, especially to Lynette, who seemed to measure every bite I put into my mouth.

When Carlotta served up second helpings, she put a dish of food at the fifth place setting.

"Is that for the guest?" I asked, remembering that when Carlotta had showed me around, she said that five rooms were occupied.

"That's our mystery guest," Lynette said. "Carlotta fixes him a plate of food every night, and every night the guy doesn't show." Lynette's words had a snap to them, like firecrackers exploding on the street.

"*Sí,*" Don Antonio said. "My sister has a heart of gold."

Lynette dropped her fork, the clanking sound of metal on china signaling the beginning of the battle. "Heart of gold?" Lynette said, making another bullet. "Wasteful is more like it!"

Studying Carlotta from across the table, her face looked smooth and relaxed. From the slow, thoughtful way she chewed her chicken, I could see that Lynette's comments did not bother her.

"How do you know it's a he?" I asked Lynette.

She shimmied in her seat, setting her elbows on either side of her dish. "Excuse me?" she asked.

"I said how do you know the guest is a man? I mean have you ever seen him?"

Lynette's face flushed red. Score one for me.

Though I hated to admit it, Daddy had taught me one thing about life. When you're the weaker one in a fight, learn quick what your opponent's weaknesses are.

"Settle down, Lynette," Carlotta said. "You look like a thermometer waiting to pop. You know that's not good for the baby."

Lynette looked at me hard, but the mention of her baby softened her a bit and she returned to shifting grains of rice around her plate.

"You see, Irena. The guest in the blue room is a very private person. He likes things done a very special way. So for this reason, you won't be responsible for cleaning his room."

Speaking before thinking, I blurted out, "So the guest is a he?"

Carlotta turned serious and I suddenly remembered the old expression, curiosity kills the cat.

"Remember, Irena. You have no reason to go anywhere near the blue room. If you do, well, I don't want to talk about that."

Dinner continued, but not as before. While Don Antonio seemed happy to gnaw on a chicken bone, everyone else turned quiet. Having narrowly missed getting hit by one of my own bullets, I reminded myself to mind my own business.

When Carlotta rose to get dessert, Don Antonio licked the chicken grease from his fingers and said, "Why don't we take our dessert outside?"

Happy to be back under the banyan, I helped Carlotta carry out the dessert. The crickets had begun their twilight concert, and the only light in the courtyard came from the flickering lanterns posted over each room's door.

Carlotta poured cups of warm milk and coffee for each of us, while I passed around a plate of homemade guava cookies.

"My room is the pink door." Carlotta pointed to the line of rooms cutting along the side of the property. "Antonio's room is the green door and Lynette's the lavender."

In the middle of the row stood my own yellow door and under me, slightly rough and scratchy against my legs, was my own yellow chair. Across the courtyard, flanked by the red- and orange-door rooms, stood the blue-door room. While curiosity might kill the cat, I wouldn't allow it to get in the way of having a new home. I promised myself not to go near the blue-door room.

Daddy had a saying. Just when you think you've pumped your balloon up to where you want it, some son-of-a-gun has to come along with the biggest, sharpest needle he can find and *whammo!*

And now, as Don Antonio set his cup down on the

ground next to him and folded his hands over his large middle, Daddy's words came back to haunt me.

"You know, Irena. Names say a lot about a person," Don Antonio said. "They can even dictate a person's destiny."

The air in my happy balloon began to seep out.

Lynette's eyes, the color of coal, fixed on me. I'd once heard that pregnant women had a sixth sense about things—a special radar of sorts. I shifted on my seat. The scratchy roughness of my chair, so comforting a minute earlier, annoyed me now.

"For instance," Don Antonio said. "My parents named me Antonio, which means priceless one."

Carlotta slapped her hand against her meaty thigh. Her booming laughter bounced off the courtyard walls as if the courtyard were a deep canyon.

"Priceless?" Carlotta huffed the words out between snorts and laughs. "*¡Una peste grande!* That's what you were. Don't listen to a word Antonio says, Irena."

"What's a *peste grande*?" Lynette asked.

"A big pest!" Carlotta said, finally catching her breath. "Even if Mama had tried giving you away, Antonio, no one would have wanted you!"

I looked at Don Antonio expecting him to be angry

with his sister, but instead, he burst out laughing. "*Sí, es verdad.* It is true," he said. "I was always into mischief."

We all laughed, and the laughter wrapped around me like a soft blanket, perfect for curling up in.

"Ah! But Papa. He was the biggest prankster of all," Don Antonio said.

"And what a liar," Carlotta added.

"A liar?" I asked. Daddy had lied to me, told me how Mama had gone away because she wanted to, but I knew this wasn't true. Daddy had made it so that Mama had had to leave.

"Oh, Papa's lies didn't hurt anyone," Carlotta explained. "He just liked to have a little fun."

Not Daddy. His lies hurt real bad. That's why I'd done what I'd done.

"A real storyteller, Papa was," Don Antonio said.

Smoothing my hand over my chair, I thought about myself, about the gator powder and running away, and the things I'd told Carlotta about Mama and Daddy. What category did I fall into? Liar or storyteller?

"I remember I was about ten years old," Don Antonio said. "Papa was sitting right here where we're sitting now. I'd been down at the docks helping the uncles bring in the nets. We used to fish for sponge back in those days," Don Antonio explained.

Don Antonio bit into his guava cookie before continuing. "We didn't have a lot of money," he said. "The uncles helped us the best they could, but we still had to scrimp and save every last penny."

"I remember those days," Carlotta said. "I could not have been more than four or five years old."

"I was starving when I came home," Don Antonio said. "But before Mama called us in for supper, Papa leaned over and told me that he'd seen Mama skinning a cat for dinner."

"That's disgusting!" Lynette said.

Though I hated to admit it, I agreed with Lynette. "What did you do when you sat down for supper?" I asked.

"Well, as I said. We were pretty poor back then, and Mama expected me to eat my dinner."

"So you ate it?" I asked.

"Stop asking so many questions," Lynette said. She was hanging so far forward in her seat I was sure she would topple over.

"I ate every last bite," Don Antonio said.

Twisting my face in disgust, I said, "Yuck!" Picking out of garbage cans was one thing, but eating a cat!

"What about Papa?" I asked.

Don Antonio's smile broadened. "Right after dinner,

he followed me outside. All he had to do was say one word and I got sick all over Mama's geraniums."

"What word was that?" Lynette asked.

"*Meow*," Don Antonio said.

Laughter started somewhere down in my toes and burst out of me like a storm cloud finally letting loose.

When we settled down, Carlotta said, "Papa was a good man. He always came through. He did so much to help us get by."

Don Antonio smiled, but Lynette sat there glumly, picking off flecks of paint from her lavender chair. She reminded me of the night I'd sat in the park, peeling off the paint from the bench.

A pleasant breeze rippled through the umbrella of leaves above us and we were quiet. A cranky mewing pierced the silence.

"Antonio! Are you teasing us again?" Carlotta asked.

Don Antonio's eyebrows rose up in an innocent arch and he said, "That wasn't me. Honest!"

The mewing continued and we all got up to search for its source.

"Up here," Lynette said, pointing into the thicket of leaves.

Don Antonio brought a ladder and a flashlight from the house. He shined the light in the direction of the mewing and there it was, the same cat I'd seen lazing beneath the banyan that afternoon.

"Is he stuck?" Lynette asked.

"Just too scared to come down, I think," Carlotta said. "He found his way up but can't find his way down."

I climbed the ladder as Don Antonio steadied it for me.

The cat resisted my first few attempts, slinking back in fear every time I reached out for it.

"Talk to it. Let it trust you," Carlotta called up to me.

"Come on, fella," I said, gently.

The cat reached out his front paw and took a timid step toward me.

"That's right," I coaxed. "You can do it."

When the cat was close enough, I clamped my hand around its thin little body, a tremble of fear rippling under my hand.

"What a sweet cat," Carlotta said, when I'd made my way down the ladder. "He must be a stray. I say we keep him."

"Just what we need. Another mouth to feed," Lynette groused.

We decided to take turns keeping the cat in our rooms. For all her grumbling, even Lynette seemed slightly pleased with this arrangement.

Holding the cat in my arms, I could feel his heart pulsing beneath his patchy fur. Daddy had always referred to cats as gator food.

"Disloyal animals," he'd once said. "Not like a dog, who sticks around."

"What should we call him?" I asked. My own heart picked up the rhythm of the little cat's.

"If you don't mind, I'd like to call him Freddie," Carlotta said, a hint of tears in her eyes.

Everyone readily agreed.

9

Although Freddie took turns sleeping with each of us, he hung around me the rest of the time. Every day, I started my job with a fresh baked roll and a glass of milk that Carlotta set out for my breakfast. As soon as Freddie saw me head into the kitchen, he trotted right behind me, loving the crumbled-up bits of roll I mashed into the milk for him.

One morning, as Freddie licked the milk from my fingers, Carlotta said, "Animals have good instincts about people, Irena. Freddie knows a good one when he sees one."

Lynette scoffed. "Oh, he's just cozying up to Irena because she always feeds him."

But I knew the real reason for Freddie's and my special relationship. It was a connection that only strays could understand.

After breakfast Freddie followed me over to the storage shed. There I gathered all the supplies I needed to do my job. Paper towels, sponges, buckets, ammonia. Carlotta liked her motel to sparkle, though Lynette forever told her she should stop buying name-brand cleaners and switch to the generic stuff, since it was cheaper.

I began in Carlotta's room. Its sweet, spicy scent always put me in a good mood first thing in the morning. Carlotta was a tidy person. I made her bed, freshened up her towels, and vacuumed, but had little else to do. Sometimes, when I took a walk, I found a pretty flower or shell and placed it on Carlotta's dresser. Carlotta had reserved a spot, next to the framed picture of her and her papa, for all the treasures I'd given her over the last month.

Picking up the picture, I looked at a young Carlotta sitting on her papa's shoulder, the two of them posing under the banyan, both with their arms bent, showing their muscles off to the camera. I'd learned from Don Antonio's stories that their papa had been a real outdoorsman and that he'd loved fishing and boxing. One look at Papa's bulging belly and mess of wavy hair would have made me run from the ring. But it was the way Carlotta's father held her, his large hand cupped around her tiny waist in a steady but gentle way, that impressed me most. Around my own father, I'd felt no steadier than a rowboat out in the middle of the ocean during a hurricane.

In Don Antonio's room, a pile of old *Life* magazines sat on his night table. Besides telling stories, Don Antonio loved reading stories, and his room was filled with books. One pile was dusty and topped by a small ceramic bust of President John F. Kennedy. Swiping the cloth over the pile, I was careful not to break anything.

A fishing cap dotted with hand-tied fishing lures sat on the dresser. Someone had scribbled something on the cap's brim, but I couldn't make out the scribbles. Old photos and postcards were taped to Don Antonio's mirror: black-and-white images of long, sandy beaches, a church with patchwork plaster, and a group of boys huddled around a soccer ball. The places and the faces did not look like any I'd seen around Key West. In one picture, Don Antonio was a teenager among a group of men—maybe the uncles he was always talking about—standing in front of a small boat called the *Esponja*, the Sponge. But the best picture was of Don Antonio and his mother. No older than three, Don Antonio sat on his mother's lap like a rare jewel she proudly showed off to the world. On the back was an inscription: *A mi hijo. Te amo, mamá.* The picture was yellowed at the edges. Don Antonio had been without his mother for such a long time.

Looking at the small silver clock on Don Antonio's dresser, I dragged myself away and headed for Lynette's room. Lynette met me at the door.

"Don't break anything, Irena. And if I find anything missing, anything at all, I'll have Carlotta fire you on the spot."

Lynette lay back on her bed, as Carlotta had advised her, with a pillow under her ankles, so puffy they resembled batter oozing out of a bread pan.

Lynette watched me work, calling out orders. "Wash the windows! Smooth the curtains! Don't forget to dust behind the toilet!"

I did what Lynette told me to do. When I reached for the vacuum I had left at the door, she stood and snatched the handle away from me. "Use this," she said, thrusting a shoddy old bristle broom at me. "Vacuuming will wear out the rugs sooner and Carlotta's already wasted enough money. She can't afford to replace the rugs too."

When I finished sweeping the sand from Lynette's carpet, I changed her sheets as she still hovered, watching everything I did. As I tucked the sheets in, I noticed something shiny hanging from her lampshade that glinted in the sunlight—a broken heart necklace, like those the kids at my old school wore when they went steady. The necklaces were sold in pairs, a charm in the shape of half a heart dangling on each chain. Without thinking, I reached for Lynette's half.

Keen as a hawk, Lynette swooped and snatched it away from me, but I had already seen the inscription: *Love*. Someone else had the other half of Lynette's heart, the *True* half.

"Remember who you are, Irena," Lynette said, tucking the necklace into her pocket.

How could I forget that I was just an outsider, especially with Lynette always reminding me.

When ignoring Lynette did no good, I decided I'd try to be her friend. One day, I found her hunched over a bowl of green beans. Sometimes she helped Carlotta with the cooking when she wasn't busy pouting over her debits and credits.

"I'll do some," I offered, sitting next to her.

"Hmmph," Lynette said, snapping her beans hard.

"Mama and I had a game," I told Lynette, trying hard to be friendly. "Whoever gets to the bottom of their pile of beans first gets to make a wish."

"So if I finish first, I can wish *you* away?" Lynette asked.

"Why doesn't Lynette like me?" I asked Carlotta the next day. She was leaning over a big skillet full of pigs' knuckles, cooking them crispy brown.

"Don't take it personally, Irena. Lynette's carrying a very big burden on her shoulders. It has nothing to do with you."

From where I stood, the burden looked like it was not on Lynette's shoulders, but settled in her belly. Every morning when she waddled to the table for breakfast, dark rings underscored her eyes. Lynette's eyes were dark as dirt to begin with, but they lacked the sparkle you can sometimes find in good, rich soil. In my lifetime I'd known only one other pregnant woman, Mama's cousin Bess. And, unlike Lynette, Bess had gloried in her pregnancy. On the first day of each month, Bess celebrated her baby's coming by dyeing her hair another color. Platinum, Auburn, Ruby Red, and Fuchsia. It got to be that people teased Bess, saying when her baby finally did pop out, the poor little thing wouldn't even recognize its own mama. But Bess shrugged the notion off, saying, "My baby's gonna know me right off because I'll be the one wearing the biggest smile!"

The only time Lynette smiled was when a group of

tourists called, looking to book a few rooms. But when they called back the next day to cancel, Lynette's smile vanished.

I didn't mind the lack of guests. The last group—students on spring break—had left their room in such a shambles, Carlotta needed to hire a handyman to repair the damage. Without outsiders coming in and making noise, the Banyan felt more like a home than a motel.

Every Friday was payday. Carlotta handed me my pay—thirty-five dollars—in a small white envelope.

"You've been cooped up here for too long, Irena," Carlotta said. "Why don't you go and buy yourself something? See the town a little?"

Rather than feeling caged in, the Banyan was my shelter, a place where I felt protected from the rest of the world. Though I didn't really care to be anywhere else, by the way Carlotta and Lynette huddled around the table, studying the ledgers, I could tell they wanted their privacy.

With my pay tucked in my pocket, I headed for Duval Street. I hadn't gone far when I stopped dead in my tracks. Parked a few yards short of the intersection at Spring and Duval was an eighteen-wheeler, the spitting image of Gabe's truck. I stepped back from the street, attempting to hide myself behind an overflowing garbage can, and I watched. When I'd ridden with him, I'd never thought to ask how often Gabe traveled to Key West and I never thought I'd have to face him again.

A blonde woman wearing coveralls crossed the street to where the rig was parked. Unlike the other tourists I'd seen, the woman walked as if she had important things to do and there was no one who was going to get in her way.

Relief washed over me when I saw the woman step up to the rig, open the door, and climb in. A minute later, the truck and the woman were gone.

Deciding to skip Duval completely, I turned instead into the alley that ran parallel to it. Aside from being safer, I liked the alleys because a lot of houses backed up to these winding paths. Slowing my pace, I peeked into the kitchen window of one of them. A little girl with springy yellow curls sat at a table waiting. Her mama came into view carrying what looked like a grilled cheese sandwich on a spatula. She laid the sandwich on the little girl's plate and gave her a peck on the cheek. A little farther down the alley, a man sat in his living room. He juggled his infant son with one hand, a paperback book in the other.

When I'd first come to Key West, watching these snippets of stories framed behind a plate of window glass made my heart ache. Some people formed families so easily, while others couldn't do it at all. But now that I'd found the Banyan, these glimpses weren't so painful to watch. Hope was pushing up out of me, the way a seedling scratches the surface of the soil before it pokes out a little green shoot.

I probably should've used my pay on a new pair of sandals, but then I remembered something.

We had just moved to the Everglades when Mama said, "Come sit with me, baby. Look what I got us."

Mama was holding a DVD.

"How'd you get that?" I asked. Since Mama didn't drive and the Everglades wasn't exactly mall country, it wasn't like Mama could just go out to a video shop and rent a movie for the night.

"A lady came by today. She bought a whole lot of trash from Will, and I helped her out to her car with the bag," Mama explained. "When I saw this movie, I said, 'I love that movie!' And the lady said she'd seen it a thousand times and why didn't I just take it."

"*Roman Holiday*?" I said, reading the title. The picture on the front showed a man and a woman. The man was riding some kind of scooter and the woman was behind him, her arms around his waist. They were both smiling and seemed to be having a real good time.

Behind them, in the distance, sat some kind of old building. It reminded me of a stadium, only a lot older and with no advertisements hanging from it.

"That's the Coliseum," Mama explained. "It's real old and very famous. It's over in Rome. That's in Italy, you know."

"Well, how do you know about it?" I asked Mama. "You ain't never been to Italy."

Mama's excited smile slipped right off her face, and I regretted my words immediately.

"That's right, Irena. I ain't been nowhere."

After that, I tried hard to paint the smile back on Mama's face. "Come on, Mama," I said. "Let's ask Will if we can borrow his DVD player."

Will obliged and Mama seemed to perk up a bit. Lucky for us too, Daddy was up in Bonita Springs picking up supplies so we could watch our movie in peace.

The movie was old, over fifty years old, but Mama didn't care. "See that, Irena," Mama said when the man kissed the woman who hated being a princess. "That's real love right there."

"I see it, Mama," I said.

After that, Mama became obsessed with the movies. Every time Will made a run to Fort Myers or Naples or

Miami, Mama slipped him a twenty and a piece of paper with a few titles scribbled on it.

"Just don't tell Dwayne," Mama would whisper to Will.

Will knew how it was between Mama and Daddy so he'd give Mama a wink and whisper back, "Anything you say, Lil."

Thinking back on that wink, I should've known then what I knew now, but I guess I didn't want to read the signals even though they were blinking right straight in my face.

Unlike Daddy, Will never disappointed, and Mama's film collection grew. She kept her movies hidden from Daddy, under the bed in a box wrapped in some moth-eaten sweaters.

"What you need these old things for, Lil?" Daddy asked Mama one day when he found the box.

"You just leave those sweaters alone, Dwayne," Mama said. "You never know when you'll be moving on to a colder climate."

Whenever Daddy went out for the night, Mama and I watched movies.

"Beautiful, beautiful," Mama would say, especially during the love scenes.

"Beautiful," I would repeat, only I wasn't really talking about the movie so much. Sitting in the dark just Mama and me, I felt safe, as if nothing else in the world mattered. Though sometimes, Mama would lean so far forward, like she wanted to jump right into the television screen, it made me feel a little uneasy.

Remembering the nice close feeling that came from watching a film in the dark, I headed for the video rental shop in Mallory Square.

The man at the shop was friendly. "If you want help, give me a call," he said, "but you have all the stuff you need right here."

"What's this?" Carlotta asked when I returned to the Banyan.

"I thought we could watch a movie tonight after dinner," I said, taking the DVD player I'd rented out of the box.

When Carlotta said, "What a wonderful idea!" my heart fluttered like a Monarch butterfly.

After dinner, Don Antonio picked up the DVD and read the title. *African Queen.* Looking at the picture of Humphrey Bogart and Katharine Hepburn gripping the rails of their little steam-powered boat, the rapids nearly jostling them overboard, Don Antonio said, "I remember some days on the *Esponja* just like it."

"Are we going to see this thing or what?" Lynette said. She'd just had another cancellation and was acting especially foul. She slumped down on one of the sky blue couches, taking nearly the entire thing for herself.

Don Antonio pushed the old console television away from the wall so that I could plug in the DVD player the way the man at the store had told me to. Carlotta set out a bowl of popcorn. In the darkness, even Lynette's sharp features softened into a smile as Rose, played by the great Kate, scowled at Charlie, played by Humphrey Bogart.

"Ah! Just let her steer the ship why don't you?" Lynnette yelled at the TV. Charlie and Rose headed down the river fleeing the German troops.

The sprig of hope wormed itself up in me again, inching steadily higher, attempting to form a thick, sturdy stem. I settled into the couch, a smile blooming on my face.

At first, I thought the burning smell I was sniffing might be coming from the burned corn kernels at the bottom of the popcorn bowl, but then Don Antonio and Lynette smelled it too. Halfway through the movie, the unimaginable happened.

"Oh!" Carlotta squealed. "Fire! The TV is on fire!"

❧ 10 ❧

The firefighters contained the damage before the fire spread.

"Here's your problem," one of them said. He pointed to the blackened outlet where I'd plugged in the DVD player. "Too many appliances plugged into one outlet. These old buildings aren't made to handle all this voltage," he explained.

The tender green shoot inside me drooped.

Lynette's moaning made me feel worse. "The bills aren't getting paid now. Where are we gonna get the money to pay for this?" She glared at me. I could tell she was calculating me right into her debit column.

Before Lynette could say another word, Carlotta

shooed us out. "It's such a beautiful night anyway. Come, Irena. You can tell us about the rest of the movie outside."

I couldn't believe it. Carlotta had almost lost her home because of me, yet she still wanted to hear about the movie.

Lynette still stewed. "I'm going to bed," she said and headed for her room. The rest of us took our chairs.

I explained the movie as I remembered seeing it the first time, with Mama. "First the village where Rose lives gets burned down and she and Charlie run away down the river on Bogie's boat," I said. "But the river is wild at some points, and it's not at all the ride Katharine Hepburn is expecting."

Don Antonio and Carlotta sat in their chairs, their eyes steady on me, listening carefully. I'd never considered myself much of a storyteller, but after listening to Don Antonio's stories about his papa and mama, I knew that details were important.

"At one point, the boat gets stuck," I said, lowering my voice to sound real dramatic. "And Charlie has to pull the *African Queen* through the reeds. But that's nothing compared to the leeches."

"Leeches?" Carlotta said, squirming slightly in her chair.

"Yep. Big black leeches, the size of my hand," I said,

holding my palm up. "As Charlie is pulling the boat through the muddy swamp, huge leeches are sticking to him, sucking the blood right out of his body!"

"Wonderful!" Don Antonio said.

"Wonderful?" Carlotta asked as if she couldn't believe her own ears. I can't say that I blamed her. What could be wonderful about leeches?

"Yes! Wonderful! I can see it like it's right there." Don Antonio pointed in front of him like he really could see the whole scene right in front of his eyes. "How is it that you can remember it so well?" he asked me.

I shrugged, but the truth was Mama and I had seen the movie so many times together that remembering the plot was as easy as breathing.

Carlotta leaned back in her chair and said, "You know, Irena, the way you tell that story reminds me of Papa. ¿No es verdad, Antonio?" Carlotta asked her brother.

Don Antonio nodded in agreement. "Yes. You are right, Carlotta. Irena's story reminds me of the stories Papa used to tell us. Papa loved to fish and he was pretty good at it too. But his fishing stories were even better—"

"And bigger!" Carlotta piped in.

"Yes, even bigger than the fish he reeled in." Don Antonio laughed.

"And whenever he returned from one of his fishing trips, he always brought us back a souvenir," Carlotta added.

Don Antonio settled back and closed his eyes. By the way he smiled, I knew he wasn't sleeping, but remembering some fond and distant memory. Don Antonio's smile was sweet and sad and woke up a bittersweet feeling in me that I'd been trying hard not to think about.

In a minute, Don Antonio's eyes blinked open and his voice had a feverishness when he spoke. "Ah! I remember the time Papa taught me to play the spoons! Do you remember, Carlotta? Yes, I got so . . . how do you say? *Frustrado.*"

"Frustrated," Carlotta translated.

"Papa could make the spoons sound like a one-man band. But I couldn't sound nearly as good as he did, no matter how much I practiced," Don Antonio said. "Then Papa finally admitted his secret."

"What was that?" I asked.

Don Antonio pointed to his right knee. "A silver kneecap, right there," he said. "Papa got it during the war. That silver kneecap made those spoons hum," Don Antonio said.

"And I sang along," Carlotta said.

"As pretty as a bird," Don Antonio said, winking at his sister. "What do you say, Carlotta? Shall we perform a little duet for our Irena?"

Our Irena. If the words hadn't been said with so much affection, I would have doubted my own ears. But the words had been said, and I drank them down in long, deep gulps.

Don Antonio went to the kitchen and returned with two teaspoons. He sat back down in his chair and gave a nod to Carlotta to begin.

Clickety, clickety, clack, clack. Clickety, clickety, clack, clack.

Don Antonio beat out a patter on his knee with the spoons and Carlotta sang:

Dentro de una flor
hay luz
cuando brilla el sol.
Dentro de una flor
hay esperanza
cuando es nueva la mañana.
Dentro de una flor
hay fuerza

cuando la tienes en tu mano.
Dentro de una flor
hay amor
cuando te doy mi corazón.

Living with Carlotta and Don Antonio, hearing Spanish every day, some of the words I hadn't understood before coming to the Banyan were now familiar. *Dentro de una flor hay luz cuando brilla el sol.* In a flower, there is light when the sun shines. *Dentro de una flor hay esperanza cuando es nueva la mañana.* In a flower, there is hope when the morning is new.

Listening to Carlotta sing, I noticed the circle we had formed—Carlotta in her pink chair, Don Antonio in his green chair, and me in my yellow chair. The circle was small, but tight, and I prayed it would never be broken and that I was the flower in Carlotta's song, a flower filled with hope and love.

The only time Lynette seemed happy was when guests checked in.

"Be sure to use the good silverware, Irena," Lynette told me as I set the table for dinner one night. Lynette refolded the napkins I had just finished folding.

"What's the big deal?" I asked Lynette. "It's only Mr. and Mrs. Strump."

"*Only* Mr. and Mrs. Strump!" Lynette repeated. "Did you see how fancy that woman was dressed when they checked in here this afternoon? If they like the Banyan, maybe they'll go back home and tell their rich friends about us."

That night, when I said, "Would you like some more wine, Mrs. Strump?" instead of saying yes, Mrs. Strump lifted her glass to the light, sniffed at the smudgy water marks, and ignored me.

"At the Four Points they have an elegant dining room," Mrs. Strump said. "French doors and cut crystal chandeliers. The waiters are very elegant. They all wear smoking jackets."

Don Antonio popped a chicken liver into his mouth. "We don't wear none of those jackets here," he said. "Didn't anyone ever tell you that smoking's bad for your health?"

"Well, yes, but . . . ," Mrs. Strump said. I could tell she did not know what to make of Don Antonio or the rest of us for that matter. She spent the remainder of the evening pushing her chicken livers around her plate.

Mr. Strump was a short bald man who seemed to suffer from the same type of sweating affliction that the preacher back home had suffered from. "I told my wife that roughing it now and then builds character. Wouldn't you say that's the case, miss?" Mr. Strump slapped Lynette on the back as if she were one of his drinking buddies from back home.

Rather than slap Mr. Strump back as I hoped she would, Lynette just sat there, smiling and nodding. For the first time since I'd arrived at the Banyan, the sight of Lynette acting so quiet and spineless made my insides curdle.

The Strumps left the next morning and first thing, I cleaned their room, hanging the pillows from the clothesline.

"What are you doing?" Lynette asked me when she saw me pounding hard at the pillows with a couple of flyswatters.

"Just airing out the room," I explained, trying to erase the smell of Mrs. Strump's expensive perfume.

At the end of May, a woman representing a needlepoint club convention called looking to reserve a block of rooms.

"They need twelve rooms," Lynette told Carlotta.

"But we only have eleven to spare," Carlotta said.

"You're forgetting the blue room, Carlotta. The blue room makes twelve," Lynette said.

Carlotta crossed her arms over her chest and said, "Absolutely not, Lynette!"

Lynette waddled off in a huff.

Later on, I offered my room for the needlepoint convention. "You and I can share a room," I told Lynette. After I said the words, I bit down hard on my tongue. Still, it was the right thing to do.

My suggestion came too little too late. The lady had already made reservations at another motel in town.

"You see!" Lynette yelled at Carlotta. "The only place your good heart is going to get us is into the poor house!"

But Carlotta just ignored Lynette. While Lynette ranted, Carlotta kneaded dough, gripping and rolling until she'd shaped the lump into a fine, long loaf.

11

Spring passed and we were already into the middle of June. It felt as if the Banyan Tree had always been my home. Each day, after I was done cleaning, I rested in my yellow chair under the shade of the banyan. The afternoon was my favorite time of the day. *Siesta,* Carlotta called it, the resting time. But while everyone else rested, I used my siesta to think.

Sitting in my chair, my head tilted back, I traced the winding branches of the banyan with my eyes. The branches all started from the same thick trunk, but then looped and turned, some reaching up, others down, for no known reason.

In my memory I saw the farmhouse in Bascom. The little house didn't look so battered now. Mama had painted the shutters and two wood boxes filled with petunias hung beneath the windows.

"I'm not going, Dwayne!" Mama yelled at Daddy.

Daddy shot out of the house. In his arms, he carried a big box.

"You've already moved us six times in three years and I'm not going to let you do it again," Mama said, following Daddy outside.

I sat on the front porch watching Daddy as he heaved that box and a whole bunch of others onto the back of our pickup. The boxes were filled with our things—pots, blankets, Mama's old transistor radio that refused to work on cloudy days. And there, on top of that pile, sat my old Raggedy Ann doll. Daddy had thrown her in, along with all the other broken things that made up our life.

"I like it here, Dwayne," Mama moaned. "At least think of Irena. How's she gonna get along down there in the swamps?"

"I am thinking of Irena," Daddy said, grabbing up another box. "Don't you get it, Lil? This job in the Everglades is big time. Mr. Everett is gonna teach me to wrestle gators."

Daddy reached for another box, and Mama balled up her hands, making two tight fists. Mama's hands were clamped so tight that the veins running under her skin bulged blue.

"Wrestling gators! Are you crazy, Dwayne?" Mama said.

"It's just like you, Lil!" Daddy said. "Always putting me down. Always saying I'm not good enough. But not this time, Lil. This time I'm gonna take a chance. This time I'm gonna get me a real profession and get ahead in the world!" Daddy had left the biggest box for last. When he picked it up he groaned from the weight. Seeing this, I couldn't help but side with Mama when she said that Daddy was crazy for wanting to wrestle gators.

"Oh, Dwayne, you are more stupid than I ever thought," Mama mocked. "It ain't like gator wrestling is the same thing as getting an MBA!"

Before we left Bascom, Mama ran up to the banyan and threw her arms around that dear tree one last time. Sitting in the truck next to Daddy, I watched as she smoothed her hands over those knobby cords, tracing the path of the tree's branches.

"What's she doin'?" Daddy wanted to know.

I shrugged, but in my heart I knew exactly what Mama was doing. That tree was just like Mama herself, starting in one place, but looking to grow in a completely different direction.

Though I still missed her, with every day that passed, sitting under the humongous canopy of this banyan tree made Mama's leaving a little bit easier to take.

One day, as I raced to put all my cleaning supplies back into the shed, I turned to look for Freddie. Normally, as I cleaned, Freddie stayed close. But where had he gone off to?

"Freddie! Freddie!" I called. "Where are you, you naughty cat?"

A patch of wild catnip grew behind the shed, but when I went to go look for him there, he was nowhere to be found.

"Freddie!" I called again, not in the mood to chase a scampy old cat. Lynette had worked me extra hard that morning, ordering me to scrub the grout in her shower with a toothbrush. I thought of how nice my yellow chair would feel, but resisted and kept looking for Freddie.

Checking under all the shrubs, I found myself standing in front of the blue room. Since coming to the Banyan, I hadn't once seen the mystery guest, though Carlotta still insisted on filling his plate every night. Sometimes, when I couldn't sleep, I cranked open the jalousie windows in my room and waited to catch a glimpse of the person staying there. Usually, I fell asleep. But on one of these nights, I spied Carlotta coming out of the blue room. How odd, I'd thought. But I didn't say anything, afraid Carlotta would think I was spying on her.

When I called out to Freddie again, this time I got an answer back.

Meow.

Stepping over a clump of ivy, I followed the sound and found myself behind the blue room gazing up at an open bathroom window. The window, identical to the window in my own bathroom, was wide enough for a nosy cat to push through but not much else.

"Here, Freddie," I said in a low voice, trying not to bother the person inside the room.

Freddie didn't so much as poke his nose out of the window.

Standing there for what seemed like forever, I listened for any noises coming from the room. Nothing. Maybe the mystery guest was out for the day.

I hadn't used my good-luck key since the day I first arrived at the Banyan, but I always carried it in my pocket. If I worked fast, I could slip into the blue room, scoop up Freddie, and be out of there before anyone found out what I was up to. I hesitated. What if Carlotta caught me? She'd told me not to mess around in the mystery guest's room.

Freddie mewed louder. Cursed cat. Not only had he gone and got himself stuck in that room, but now I was stuck too.

Lucky for me, it was late afternoon. Surely Carlotta was busy in the kitchen chopping ingredients for that night's dinner. Don Antonio was taking his afternoon siesta, and Lynette was nowhere to be seen.

Trying to hang back in the bushes that framed the room's door, I worked the key fast, fishing around for the tiny spot that would release the lock's mechanism. After a minute of wiggling and probing, I was beginning to worry that I'd lost my knack. But then, *click!* The lock turned over. Making sure that no one had noticed, I shoved the door slightly, opening it.

The blinds were drawn and the room was almost black except for a single shaft of light coming from the bathroom window. I resisted turning on the light.

I imagined the blue room to be laid out like all the other rooms at the motel, and, getting down on my hands and knees, I began to crawl. "Freddie!" I called out in a whisper.

"Ow!" I reached out in front of me and felt around

in the dark, trying to figure out what I'd just bumped my head on. Something large and smooth sat in the middle of the room. Whatever it was, someone had draped a sheet over it. Other things about the room seemed out of place too. The carpet felt softer than the carpet in any of the other rooms, and there was an odor of fresh paint.

"Freddie!"

My hands grazed something fuzzy. Freddie? No. Only a pair of slippers.

Then I found him, snug in the corner of the room where the dresser should have been. "Fool cat," I said, hugging him to my chest as I backed out of the mystery guest's room.

Once outside, I locked the door, but as I did this, the hairs on the back of my neck stood up as straight as cattails on a breezy day.

"And what exactly are you doing?"

It was Lynette, her coal black eyes boring into me. Holding Freddie tight in my arms, I wished he was a ferocious lion and not the fool cat he really was.

"Didn't Carlotta warn you to keep out of this room?" Lynette said. "And didn't she tell you what would happen if you didn't?"

I stood there shuddering in the warm sunlight.

Actually, Carlotta had never said exactly what she'd do if she found me in the mystery guest's room, but I wasn't willing to find out. Carlotta had already forgiven me for the fire, but what if her heart was only so big and her forgiveness only went so far?

Lynette must have sensed this fear in me for she said, "I'll tell you what, Irena. I won't tell Carlotta about you trespassing if you tell me what you saw in there."

"Nothing," I said. "It's just a room. Same as all the other ones," I lied.

But Lynette wasn't buying my lies. "Don't cross me, Irena, 'cause you'll be sorry if you do," Lynette threatened.

Lynette was like a fisherman who'd hooked me good. But if I was patient and didn't wiggle too much, I might be able to unhook myself and swim free for another day.

"Well, there is one strange thing about that room," I said, trying to keep my wits about me.

"Yes? What? Tell me!" Lynette demanded.

I used the only thing I had. I said, "Paint! I smelled fresh paint when I went into the room."

"Paint?" Lynette said, mulling this little tidbit over in her mind.

"Maybe the person is an artist," I suggested.

"Sugar snaps!" Lynette puffed.

I couldn't help but giggle. The way Lynette said *sugar snaps*, like a prissy little kindergarten girl, made her sound downright silly.

"Oh, so you think this is funny," Lynette fumed. "The only thing this guy is doing is stealing us blind. Carlotta lets him stay free of charge when she could rent the room out and make money."

Opening my mouth, I quickly shut it, fearful of getting hooked again. What I wanted to say was that if Carlotta let someone live here for free, wasn't it her choice? But when it came to money, there was no reasoning with Lynette.

Finding me sneaking out of the mystery guest's room was, for Lynette, like discovering a winning lottery ticket.

"How's about this, Irena?" Lynette's bangs fell jaggedly across her forehead as if she hadn't had the patience to sit still in the chair while the barber tried to cut them. "I won't let Carlotta know you've been snooping in places you're not supposed to, if you do me a little favor."

I couldn't believe it! Lynette wasn't letting me loose no matter what I did or said. Then I remembered something the preacher had once said during Sunday services. "No man shall rob your key to the gates of heaven!"

The preacher had never met Lynette.

12

"You want me to what?" I asked Lynette.

"I want you to follow Carlotta," Lynette said.

"Why would you want me to do something like that?"

"I have my reasons."

We stood in the middle of Lynette's dark room. The only hint of light came through gaps in the blinds. It reminded me of an old spy film I'd once seen with Mama, only this time I was the one being forced to do something against my will, not Robert Redford.

"Why can't you do it?" I asked.

"What, are you kidding?" Lynette said, pointing at her huge stomach.

It was true. Over the last few weeks, Lynette's profile was looking more and more like Alfred Hitchcock's.

As Lynette plowed through her desk drawer looking for something, I glanced around her room. A rabbit, made from some kind of soft, nubby material, sat on her night table. The price tag dangled from its ear. $4.95. How had stingy old Lynette built up the nerve to plunk her precious money down?

Lynette shoved a pencil and small notebook at me. "Here! Take these and write down everywhere Carlotta goes."

I took the pencil and the notebook. "But why?" I asked again.

"Just do it!" Lynette sniped back. Her pinched face could've made a gator turn tail.

When she was done with me, Lynette pushed me out of her room and into the sharp afternoon sun. The contrast from dark to light stung my eyes, and, for a minute, everything looked fuzzy and out of focus, as if it were a dream.

Freddie came up from behind me, grazing my foot. A reminder of how I'd gotten into this mess in the first place.

"*Meow,*" Freddie said.

"Oh, all right. You're forgiven," I said. After all, Freddie was a cat. It wasn't fair to hold a grudge against him for doing what came naturally to him—finding mischief.

I picked Freddie up in my arms. He'd gained weight since arriving at the Banyan and his fur smelled fresh, a mixture of sunshine and soap. Carlotta insisted on bathing Freddie, even though Lynette thought it was a complete waste of time.

"Everyone knows cats clean themselves and they hate water," she said one day as Carlotta lifted Freddie into the kitchen sink.

"Oh, Lynette," Carlotta said, pooh-poohing Lynette's comment. She added a small drop of baby shampoo to the palm of her hand and began gently rubbing the shampoo into Freddie's coat.

"He's a stray! What does it matter to him?" Lynette said.

"All living things know what makes them happy," I said. "Even though other people might think otherwise."

Lynette glared at me, but Carlotta said, "Very true, Irena." Then she poured a cup of warm water over Freddie's head, releasing the suds from his coat. Freddie sat in the sink, purring happily and enjoying Carlotta's attention.

But the words I'd spoken were Will's, not mine. When he'd said them, he'd been talking about Mama, trying to bring me comfort after she left. I supposed it applied to cats too.

I stood there awhile petting Freddie. When he became bored with my caresses, he wiggled out of my arms. I watched as he trotted away toward a sparrow perched on one of the low branches of the banyan. Freddie's step was springier now, not so sluggish the way it had been when he first showed up at the motel. Amazing what a good home and love could do for an animal or any living thing, for that matter.

I couldn't sleep that night. If Carlotta caught me, she would never trust me again. And if I refused, Lynette would snitch. Either way my hands were tied. The same thing happened every time Daddy announced we were moving. Just when I got used to a place, he pumped up the trailer tires and started fingering a map.

Well, I was tired of following blindly, jumping whenever someone told me to jump. What had it gotten me in the past besides a tired heart and two sore feet?

So the next morning, I marched into Lynette's room and said, "I just won't do it!"

Lynette sat there quietly, picking at the white foam that poked out of her seat cushion, not saying a word. Her silence seemed to last for days and by the time I finally got my courage up to speak again, a small pile of foam lay crumbled at Lynette's feet.

"I'm no good at spying," I told Lynette. "And I don't really know my way around Key West." Even I could tell how clumsy and false my excuses sounded.

"You didn't have a problem finding your way here, did you?" Lynette said.

The debate was over. Lynette's words were sharper and fiercer and she hadn't even raised her voice.

Lynette rattled off Carlotta's schedule. As she spoke, she rubbed her belly. Pity filled me. When Cousin Bess was pregnant, she let anyone touch her stomach on account of she wanted her baby to know just how friendly the world could be. But now, as Lynette told me where Carlotta did her shopping and when she went to the hairdresser, I doubted Lynette trusted the world in quite the same way.

Even in the middle of my own misery, something needled me like a splinter and I just needed to know. "Do you have a name picked out for the baby?" I asked Lynette.

"Vera," Lynette said. And without skipping a beat, she said, "Carlotta usually goes to the market, but after that she heads for who knows where."

I pretended to listen, but instead thought about the

old-fashioned name. In all the movies Mama and I had seen together, Vera Miles was the only movie star with such a frumpy name. Real stars had exotic names like Greta or Grace. If Don Antonio was even the least bit right about the key to your destiny being found in your name, Lynette's kid didn't have a chance.

And what if the baby wasn't a girl? Lynette could control other people better than the ringmaster at the circus, but she didn't have the power to choose the sex of her own child. Did she?

Lynette shook my shoulder. "Get your head out of the clouds. Carlotta goes out every morning after she finishes the breakfast dishes and you'd better be ready."

Lynette pointed to a spot where I could wait for Carlotta without being seen. Wedged between a rotting fence post and the shed, I felt like a dog waiting for a little kid to drop her lollipop.

Carlotta showed up a half hour later carrying a straw purse. Her vibrant orange dress made her skin glow the same color as her caramel-colored jam. When she turned down Spring Street in the direction of the Gulf, I followed.

Spying, it turned out, wasn't very hard as long as you kept your distance and acted natural, like you were supposed to be there. When Carlotta stepped into the market, I hung back at the shoe shop a couple of stores down. I thought I blended in until the salesman at the shop eyed me. Confused, I finally understood his gaze when I realized I was holding a pair of lemon yellow cowboy boots.

When Carlotta finished at the market, she walked clear across town toward the commercial fishing docks. The docks lay along the northeast banks of Key West, a part of town I'd never much liked. The pretty cottages and shops on the south side of town, where families and tourists mingled on never-ending holiday, were my favorites.

Warehouses lined the docks, some rundown and abandoned, others still bustling with the sounds of workers and machinery. Carlotta ducked into one of them, and I hid behind an overturned sailboat, giving her some time to sink into the place before I sneaked up closer.

I eased in. A thin coat of dried salt filmed the windows, making everything inside look soft and out of focus. I finally made out Carlotta's hefty shape through the dirty glass. She was talking to a man dressed in work overalls. He pointed to a pallet of wood and said something I couldn't hear over the shrill screams of drills and electric saws. Carlotta nodded back to the man and then drew her wallet from her purse. From where I stood, I couldn't see how much money she gave him, but the thick stack of bills must have been quite a sum.

The man shook Carlotta's hand, ending their business together. I turned to go before Carlotta found me, but my foot caught in a fishing net left on the docks to dry. Like a bear caught in a trap, I struggled to release my foot. The more I pulled, the more tangled up I became. I heard voices. Carlotta was coming! Soon she'd find me and then what? What explanation could I give for being there?

I tugged again and just as Carlotta exited the warehouse, I freed my foot. Quickly, I scampered behind a pile of old buoys.

"Thank you again," I heard Carlotta say.

My heart beat so loudly that I was sure the sound of it might echo off the aluminum walls of the warehouse.

"Any time," the man told Carlotta.

I sat behind the buoys, not moving until I knew for sure that Carlotta was gone. Then I remembered the notebook Lynette had shoved at me. The warehouse had a sign—FRANK'S FINE FURNITURE. I scrawled the name down in the notebook. It wasn't much, but this small bit of information might cool Lynette down long enough for me to consider my next step.

I wandered around town, giving Carlotta plenty of time to get back to the Banyan. I did this to give Carlotta her space, but also figured that once Lynette discovered that I hadn't discovered much of anything, she might go easier on me if Carlotta was within earshot.

I found a used bookstore. The store was dark and cat hair settled in small mounds on the shelves, but there was something comforting about the musty old smell of books. A woman sat at the front desk. Her wire-rimmed glasses matched the color of her silver hair. She smiled at me, then returned to her book. As she read, she laughed. She enjoyed her job. A pang of fear and sadness washed over me. I knew how it felt to really love my job, and I had to find a way to keep it.

I lingered in Mysteries, reading the plots on the backs of the Agatha Christies. I recognized some of the stories from movies I'd seen. Romance was the next section. The covers on these books were all the same—beefy musclemen embracing big-bosomed starlet types. I looked at those women with their wild hair blowing in the wind. Their necks should have just bowed over from the weight of those tresses.

I moved down the stacks, concentrating hard on the categories. Philosophy, Psychology, New Age. All books meant to help people with their problems. Somehow I doubted the answer to my problem could be found anywhere in those books.

One shelf up front displayed books only by Ernest Hemingway.

The lady behind the counter noticed me looking at the display. "Our most popular author. Half the books we sell are by him," she said.

Remembering the house on Whitehead Street, I wondered what the fascination was with this guy. One book, *The Old Man and the Sea,* pictured a white-bearded fisherman reeling in a monstrous swordfish. The picture reminded me of Don Antonio's tales about fishing with his father. I thought about buying the book, but changed my mind. No matter how good a writer Ernest Hemingway might be, no one could beat one of Don Antonio's stories.

At the end of the row sat a big box of paperbacks. Picking over the odd collection that included *Cooking with Your Mother-In-Law and Loving It* and *Pajamas Are for Everyone,* I found a book called *The Name Game.* Flipping through the section for girls' names, I found my own: *Irena—Greek for "peace." Very common under the Roman Empire; first appeared in English-speaking countries in the mid-nineteenth century.*

Hot tears stung my eyes. Mama's leaving had left me with so many unanswered questions, and, even though I had no more answers than before, finding Carlotta and

Don Antonio had given me a feeling of peace I hadn't had before coming to the Banyan.

The lady at the counter glanced up at me and I quickly wiped my face.

"I'm allergic to dust," I explained.

"I see," the woman said, returning again to her book.

I turned to the section marked "V" and looked up the meaning for Vera.

Vera—Latin for "true." Popular in the nineteenth century, the name is hardly found now.

Staring at the entry, I remembered the necklace hanging from the lampshade in Lynette's room and I wondered.

13

Frank's Fine Furniture! Frank's Fine Furniture!" Lynette read the words as if they were a tongue twister.

"That's all the sign said," I explained. My spine itched with fear, and I could hardly resist scratching it.

"Did it ever occur to you to go in and ask what type of furniture Frank makes?" But Lynette didn't wait for an answer. She flung the notebook across the room.

Something deep inside me, not in my control, flinched. A memory of other things being tossed across the room, loud shouting, slamming doors, and leaving popped inside me. I pushed down real hard on those memories, trying to shove them out of my head.

"You think how Carlotta spends her money is none of my business, don't you?" Lynette pressed me.

"Not really," I said. The words dribbled out pathetically.

"No, but that's what you were thinking. Weren't you?"

Shrugging my shoulders, I figured it was best not to say anything lest Lynette fling me across the room too.

Lynette plopped down on the bed, her weight pressing the thin mattress almost to the level of the box spring.

"Here," I said, handing her the name book. I'd bought it for her as a peace offering of sorts. "I thought you might like to know what your baby's name means."

Lynette glared at me, but took the book anyway. As she read, little lines like raccoon tracks fanned out from the corners of her eyes. I'd always thought that only older people got those lines, but then again, a lot about Lynette seemed older.

"That's nice," Lynette said, reading what Vera meant. She sat there, staring at the sun dust floating in through the window, and then she added, "Vera is Mike's last name."

"Who's Mike?" I asked.

"Vera's daddy."

"Vera's daddy?" The idea tugged at my funny bone and I couldn't help but snicker.

"What's so funny?" Lynette scowled.

"Oh, nothing," I said, trying to hold myself back. "It's just that, if you name your baby Vera, her name will be Vera Vera."

Lynette's eyes turned murky black. "It's not gonna work that way," she said. "Mike doesn't plan on giving Vera his last name or anything else for that matter. He won't even admit that this is his baby."

For the first time I realized why Lynette held herself so tight. She probably thought that if she didn't, she just might shatter into a million pieces.

"At least Vera has you," I blurted out. "And there's Carlotta and Don Antonio. And me too."

Lynette shook her head, her stick-straight hair falling in a sheet like a heavy downpour of rain. "Oh, Irena. There's so much you don't know."

She was right. There was so much I didn't know, like why Mama had left me. Me! When I had been the one to always break Mama's fall whenever she felt like she was tumbling through life, when I'd been the one to put myself between her and Daddy that night.

"It's not that I think you're bad or anything," Lynette told me. "It's just that you're another mouth to feed and, well . . ." She wrung her hands, forming red splotches on her white, white skin. "Irena, you're not the one doing the books. You don't see what I see."

I was finally getting the picture. "You're talking about money," I said.

Lynette corrected me. "The Banyan's money. At the rate Carlotta is spending, the bank is going to foreclose on the Banyan for sure."

"But what about the money from guests?" I asked.

"Have you seen any guests coming in and out of here lately?" Lynette asked.

It was true. Other than the Strumps, the Banyan had been very quiet.

"It's just the slow season," I told Lynette. "Once the winter comes, I'm sure we'll fill up."

"Winter is months away and it might be too late by then. Besides, with all the other motels on Key West, the Banyan hardly stands out."

"Have you talked to Carlotta and Don Antonio about it?" I asked.

"Sure I have. Don Antonio says Carlotta will handle it, and Carlotta says God will handle it. Meanwhile, nobody's handling anything and we're getting deeper and deeper into debt."

I looked at Lynette. The baby had made her as thick as an old tree around the middle. What I was realizing was that, like an old tree, she was rough on the outside, but her inside was smooth. Now I saw. Lynette and I were more the same than different. A dull, sad ache rose up inside me. It was hard enough at my age not knowing where you belonged. What about the baby?

"Now what do we do?" Lynette sighed. "I've staggered the bill payments, but sooner or later the bank is going to catch up with us."

I teetered on the edge of Lynette's bed. Something had shifted between her and me. Like every time we drove the trailer from one town to another and things fell out of the cabinets. One time, after one of those trips, we spent two weeks looking for a can of baked beans before we found it. But losing the Banyan was a heck of a lot different from losing a can of baked beans.

"How much time till the money runs out?" I asked.

"A month or two. Not much more."

Counting in my head, a month would put Lynette in the eighth month of her pregnancy.

As if she could read my mind, Lynette said, "All I ever wanted to do was give my baby a home."

Slumped next to Lynette, I flipped through the name book over and over again. All those names. People all over the world had those names. There had to be someone who could help us.

14

Over the next few weeks, I offered my ideas for saving the Banyan. Lynette immediately shot them down.

"We can advertise," I suggested.

"Advertising costs money," Lynette said.

"We can have a dinner theater and put on a show!"

"Sure, sure," Lynette said. "You and Freddie can sing off-key and I'll dance with my swollen ankles."

"I could give you the money Carlotta pays me every week," I said.

Lynette really got a kick out of this last suggestion. "Thanks for the offer," she said. "But keep the pocket change."

I thought of calling Will for advice. "He's a shrewd one, he is," Daddy always used to say. Will was shrewd and not just about business, but phoning Will would've opened a whole other can of worms that would only make my situation worse.

I was out of ideas but not out of hope.

"There has to be something we can do to attract customers," I told Lynette one afternoon as I washed the lunch dishes and she dried them. Lynette was quiet, fretting over the helping of carne asado Carlotta had ladled into a bowl for the mystery guest.

"I just don't get it," she said. She was drying a terracotta bowl so furiously, I wouldn't have been surprised if she had stripped the glaze right off. "Why is Carlotta letting him get away with it?" she wanted to know.

"Maybe she's so desperate she feels like she doesn't have any other choice," I volunteered. I was talking about Carlotta. Well, at least, I thought I was talking about Carlotta. The memory of Mama hung over me. Even when I wasn't thinking about her, she still managed to cast a shadow over my life.

"Desperate about what?" Lynette asked.

"Aw, I don't know," I said, wondering why people were so darn hard to figure out. "Anyway. Who cares? We need to think up a way to get more customers."

Though I didn't admit it to Lynette, the idea of the mystery guest bothered me too. To make things worse, every time I turned around that week, I found Carlotta sneaking into the motel carrying another bag.

"She knows she should be saving money," Lynette moaned. "But she still goes out shopping like everything is peaches and cream!"

I thought about talking to Carlotta, but then hesitated because of something she'd said to me that morning as we sorted through the dried black beans she planned to cook for dinner.

"You know, Irena. I hope you understand how welcome you are here."

I sat there running my hands over my plate of beans, picking through to find a tiny pebble or a grain of dirt. A tough task, especially behind a veil of tears.

How could I even consider questioning Carlotta? If I dared, I knew everything would change, the same way it does when you look at a picture you like for too long. At first, you enjoy the picture, but then you start seeing little faults in it, like how the color of the water isn't quite right or the tree is way too small compared to the house. My heart wasn't quite ready to see Carlotta's imperfections.

Working at Will's had taught me a thing or two about running a business. The most important thing was to give the customers something they couldn't get any-where else and to let them think that they were in a place like no other. I already knew the Banyan was special, but how could I make other people believe the same thing?

"You want to take me where?" Lynette asked when I told her my idea.

"To the Hemingway house," I said.

"What for?" Lynette asked. She sat down to listen. Lately, even something as easy as drying dishes tired her out.

"They get a lot of people coming to visit and taking their tours. Maybe we can get some ideas from them on how to attract more customers," I said.

Lynette rubbed her ankles as she thought. "Heming-way was some kind of writer, huh?"

"Yeah. Good enough to have a section of his own in the bookstore," I said.

"Mike used to write me love poems when we were dating. He thought he was darn good, told me he'd been published in his school paper," Lynette said. She jutted out her lower lip and patted her belly. "It would fix him good to know that I've been to Hemingway's house."

I didn't quite understand the connection Lynette was making, but I was glad she was up for the idea.

The next day was Friday—payday—and after I did

my chores and Lynette finished paying another stack of bills, we headed over to the Hemingway house.

Waiting in line to pay our entrance fee, I pointed to an elderly man taking tickets at the ticket booth. "Check him out," I whispered to Lynette. The man sat slightly hunched as he doled out change to a customer. A gray and white tabby cat tiptoed across his shoulders as if it was walking a tightrope.

Two of the people ahead of us were talking about the cat. "That's one of Hemingway's famous six-toed cats," one of them said.

"Do you think we can teach Freddie that trick?" I asked Lynette.

"Freddie yes. Don Antonio? He's another story," Lynette said.

I plunked down sixteen dollars for Lynette and me. The man handed us two pamphlets. Lynette grabbed up both, stuffing them into the pocket of her shorts. "We can read later. Let's get this show on the road. My back is killing me."

In the past week, Lynette's ankles had swollen even more and her back had begun to hurt terribly. Lynette promised Carlotta she would go see the doctor, but she put off the visit, saying she had better things to do with her money.

Once we'd paid for our tickets, we were allowed past the tall wall. Hemingway's house was a pretty two-story building with a wooden wraparound porch on the first floor and a wrought-iron veranda on the second floor.

The tour guides staggered their tours, the same way Will staggered his airboat rides every fifteen minutes so people had time to explore and not bump into one another.

"We'll be getting started in a few minutes, folks. Enjoy the gardens while you wait," our tour guide told us. The man was tall and peppy with freckles on his knees to match the ones on his face. His shirt was printed with orange and yellow birds of paradise.

"I like that shirt he's wearing," I told Lynette. "It's bright, and the tourists will always know where he is."

"No chance of losing that fool," Lynette sniped. She'd found a bench and was massaging her ankles.

"Come on, Lynette," I urged. "This is a chance for us to learn!"

"To learn what? How stupid we really are? Look, Irena. I know you're trying really hard, but I don't see how any of this is going to help us."

Looking around at the pretty palms and fancy house, my heart slumped. Maybe Lynette was right. I hadn't even been in Hemingway's house yet, and I could already tell that this place had something the Banyan didn't. Sitting next to Lynette, I watched a troop of tourists snake along the upstairs veranda. Even from where we were sitting, I could hear the crowd laughing at the well-rehearsed tour guide.

"It's our turn," our tour guide said. He waved us on to follow him through the main entrance of the house.

But Lynette didn't move. She just sat there looking whiter than chalk, and she was sweating.

"Are you okay?" I asked her.

"Sure, sure. I'm fine. Just go on without me," she said.

Our group was already in the entrance. The tour guide was talking and pointing to something I couldn't make out.

"Go on! I'll be fine," Lynette said. Little beads of sweat dotted her upper lip.

The image of Mama walking away played out in my head. I'd trusted her to be strong, but she turned her back on me just the same. I didn't have the heart to do the same to Lynette.

All the way back to the Banyan, Lynette grumbled about the sixteen dollars we'd lost. "Good money down the drain and a total waste of time!"

15

Lynette stretched out on the couch and complained. "I can't just sit here for the next two months!"

"You can and you will," Carlotta said. She fluffed up a pillow and propped it up behind Lynette.

Lynette looked at me to save her, but I didn't say a word. When we returned that afternoon, Carlotta had taken one look at Lynette and phoned the doctor. Complete bed rest. That's what the doctor ordered after he'd examined Lynette.

When Carlotta went to look for more pillows, Lynette leaned over and whispered, "Now what? With me flat on my back, how are you going to handle things?"

Thinking back to the way I'd handled things with Daddy and Will, using that gator powder as a way out and as a way to get even, I didn't see how that kind of strategy would apply to the mess the Banyan was in. But looking at Lynette, her bangs clinging to her sweaty forehead, I knew I had to stay confident. "Everything's going to be fine. You'll see," I said and then I plastered a big fake smile across my face.

June passed into July and nothing changed. One night I helped Carlotta in the kitchen while Don Antonio entertained us with Papa stories. Lynette, insisting that she couldn't bear to sit for one more second on the couch, had compromised with Carlotta and was now sitting on the La-Z-Boy Don Antonio had brought into the kitchen for her.

"Papa loved to box," Don Antonio said. "He was a big man, muscular too. If he wasn't out at sea struggling to pull in a big marlin, he was looking for someone to take him on in the ring."

"Did you ever fight him?" Lynette asked.

Don Antonio shook his head and chuckled. "Me? No. I was too young, and as Papa said, I didn't have the heart of a fighter."

"So Papa knew what it took to win a fight?" I asked, looking at Lynette.

As usual, Lynette's black eyes bore into me, but this time, I knew, the intensity behind her stare had nothing to do with me.

"Oh, yes. Papa knew how to win. But he also knew how to bow out gracefully when it was necessary," Don Antonio said.

"How's that?" Lynette asked.

"Well, there was this fellow by the name of Bill," Don Antonio said. "Nice young man. Papa thought the world of him."

"Ah! Bill," Carlotta said, chiming in. "Nice man. Very nice."

"So what happened?" I wanted to know.

"Papa and Bill sparred together until one day when Bill hit Papa in the nose and drew blood," Don Antonio said.

"Was your papa all right?" I asked. As soon as the words slipped out of my mouth, I knew I wasn't only wondering about Don Antonio's papa. Lately, I'd been wondering about Daddy, feeling bad about the gator powder and hoping I hadn't done anything too bad to him.

"Oh, Papa was fine," Don Antonio said and then he laughed. "But after that he told Bill that they'd be better off if they didn't box anymore, since they were friends, after all."

As I chopped onions and green peppers for Carlotta's famous black bean soup, thoughts swam around my head like sharks in a frenzy. When was it time to put up a fight for what you wanted and when was it time to give up?

"For the best black beans, you have to make the onions sweat first," Carlotta explained. The slivered white onions turned clear and soft in the pan and Carlotta gave me the go-ahead to add the peppers.

Carlotta tilted her head over the pan and breathed in the vapor. "Hmm . . . nice," she said as if the peppers and onions were some rare, exotic perfume.

It was nice. All of it. Not just Carlotta's black bean soup, but Don Antonio's stories, Carlotta's loving, and even Lynette's groaning. We were like the ingredients in Carlotta's soup. Together we were better than anything we could ever be on our own.

The phone rang. I stirred the onions and peppers while Carlotta answered it.

She cupped her hand over the receiver. "Irena, dear. Turn the heat down on the burner." And then Carlotta took the phone into the living room.

As Don Antonio began another story, I moved toward the doorway between the kitchen and the living room. Though Carlotta was speaking in a low voice, I picked up a few words.

After dinner, I told Lynette what I'd heard.

"Are you sure?" Lynette asked.

"I'm positive," I said, wishing more than anything that I wasn't.

"And she was asking the person for more time?" Lynette said.

"'Can't you give us a little more time,'" I said, repeating word for word what I'd heard Carlotta say.

Lynette looked pale and tired.

"What is it? Don't you feel well?"

"It's not the baby," Lynette said. "Don't you see, Irena? That person Carlotta was talking to was from the bank. I bet they've started foreclosure proceedings on us."

Time. Carlotta had asked for more of it. But even if we had more time, would that give us what we needed to save the Banyan?

The next day Carlotta asked me to run an errand for her. I was to bring a package to a lady who worked at a cigar shop in town.

Before I left, Lynette pulled me aside. "It's bad, Irena. Remember the person who called last night? He's coming today to talk to Carlotta."

"How do you know? Did Carlotta tell you?"

"No. I overheard her talking this morning on the

phone. She told whoever it was on the other end that his visit would disrupt all our lives. She asked him to wait a little longer to give her a chance to settle things."

Settle things? How did Carlotta plan to do that?

"What's in the package?" Lynette asked.

"Huh?" I said, wondering who the person was who was coming that evening. "Oh, this? Something Carlotta wants me to deliver," I said. Carlotta had carefully wrapped the package in brown paper and twine.

"Well, as long as it's for Carlotta and not for you-know-who," Lynette said, gesturing in the direction of the blue room. She was still fuming over the mystery guest. The night before, at dinner, Carlotta had filled the mystery guest's bowl with a double helping of black bean soup and sausages. The food turned gloppy and cold when no one showed up to eat it.

I promised Lynette I'd be back in time.

"Safety in numbers," Lynette said to me as I headed to do Carlotta's errand. Funny how, in war, enemies become friends just like that.

The cigar shop was tucked away into an alley off Duval. The walls of the shop were lined with shelves the color of milk chocolate. On the shelves were humidors filled with cigars and cigarillos.

"Hello," I called out. A black cat nestled on one of the shelves pawed at the air as if to say hello back.

A stout woman appeared through a blue-and-yellow-striped curtain that hung at the back of the shop. "May I help you?" she asked.

"I'm looking for Doña Teresa," I explained. "I have a package for her."

She gestured for me to follow her.

In the narrow back room, Doña Teresa didn't bother looking up from the small wooden table where she worked rolling cigars.

"Doña Teresa." The woman spoke loudly, startling another cat that lazed in a patch of sunlight by the back door.

Was Doña Teresa deaf? She looked up, squinting, her hands still rolling the tender tobacco leaf.

"Carlotta asked me to give this to you," I said. The woman pointed her chin in my direction, eyeing me in the same way she might check a tobacco leaf to see if it was good enough. Instead of speaking, Doña Teresa dipped her finger into a small glass of water, ran it over the end of the leaf, then sealed the cigar with a small paper band. The band was dark brown, darker than the tobacco leaf itself. The gold letters on the band shone. It had the name of the shop printed on it and below that, the words *hand-rolled by Doña Teresa.*

So it wasn't her hearing but the old woman's arrogance that made her ignore me. I felt that arrogance now in every nook of the small dark room. It seemed to suck the air right out of the place.

Doña Teresa finally took the package from me. She cut the twine and tore at the brown paper, revealing a set of linen napkins. Each napkin had a different flower embroidered on it, each stitch carefully placed. Whoever had sewn them had taken a great deal of care.

But all Doña Teresa could do was wrinkle up her nose. "Tell Carlotta I would never sell such garbage in my store. What does she take me for? She should feel ashamed of herself for trying to pass off her shoddy needlework."

Her needlework? Carlotta had embroidered these napkins?

Doña Teresa threw the napkins back into the torn wrapping and shoved them at me.

"But the check," I said, suddenly remembering. "Carlotta told me you would pay me."

"If you're looking for money, you've come to the wrong place," she sneered. "Tell Carlotta she'll get no money out of me!"

The thick smell of tobacco burned the inside of my nose and left my stomach sour. At the end of the narrow room the back door led out to the street. I nodded and quickly walked out that door, not wanting to spend a minute longer with the awful woman.

I found myself back on Duval Street, just across from the churchyard where I'd slept my first week in Key West. Funny how I'd never noticed the cigar shop, but from this side of the street, the shop was nothing more than a hole in the wall.

Holding up Carlotta's napkins, I examined them more closely in the sunlight. A lily, an iris, a daisy. Each flower was perfect. Why would Carlotta want her napkins displayed in such an ugly place? And worse, why would she so willingly hand over her precious work to an ogre like Doña Teresa? Then I thought of the check I was meant to collect and it began to make sense. As much as Carlotta pretended not to worry, she was just as scared as Lynette and I. She didn't want to lose the Banyan, and these napkins were her small attempt to save it.

I crossed the street, passing the spot where I'd slept. The spot was grown over and weedy now.

For the first time, I made my way into the church. It was the same warm color as the cigar shop on the inside, but the church was large with a clear story of windows where the walls and the ceiling met. I felt welcome there. I shuffled into the closest pew.

The movies always show angels all light, their wings wispy like they're fashioned from two high-quality feather dusters. So when the priest came up behind me, slight and looking like some gangly kid who should've been out playing basketball, I never considered that he might be in the business of salvation.

"Are you okay, child?" he asked. "Do you have something there that needs looking after?"

I had no idea what the priest was getting at until I saw that he was staring down at the bundle in my arms.

"Oh, no," I said. "This isn't what you think." I showed him the napkins, and he laughed, a rosy shade of pink working its way up his neck to his cheeks.

"My mistake," he said, chuckling at himself.

Though he wore the same collar the traveling preacher had worn, this priest seemed different to me.

"Could I ask you something, Father?" I said.

The priest sat down next to me and said, "Ask away!"

What was I doing? This guy didn't seem much older than Lynette. What did he know about the world when he probably spent most of his time holed up in the church praying to a god that was a lot better at listening than he was at answering questions? But this priest had a smooth, peaceful face, and a quick assessment of his armpits told me that he was more pure of heart than the traveling preacher.

I must've been holding my breath forever because the words came out of me in one long exhalation. "Why are people always messing up?" I asked. "I mean . . . why do people do things even when they know those things are wrong?"

The priest looked down at his fingers, but didn't say anything. His nails were short and clean. Too clean for playing basketball. I sat there squirming, feeling stupid at having misjudged him.

He cleared his throat, and I waited for his words of wisdom. "We know only God is perfect," the priest said.

"Yes, only God," I repeated, holding on to this nugget and waiting.

"The rest of us are pretty much screwed up, though doing the best we can with what we've got," the priest added, and then he went back to looking at his fingers.

"That's it?" I asked. I'd never spoken to a man of the cloth like this before, but surely there had to be more to it.

"That's pretty much it," the young priest said. I couldn't fault him for his lack of wisdom really, but I couldn't help but feel disappointed for the second time that day.

"Can I take a look at those?" the priest asked. He took a napkin and ran his fingers over the stitches. "Pretty," he said. "They remind me of my grandmother."

While he wasn't good with answers, there was something about the young priest that made me feel comfortable asking more questions.

"Father," I said, still feeling sort of silly calling this young man *father*. "Does this church have a gift shop by any chance?"

"Why, yes, we do," he said.

"Would you sell these napkins in your gift shop?" I asked. And then I quickly added, "Of course the church would get a small commission from each sale."

"These things would fly off the shelves!" he said. How funny to hear a priest talking like a businessman. In my head, I began to calculate how much money we could make embroidering napkins if Lynette and I both helped Carlotta.

"I'll tell you what," the priest said. "I'll take the whole lot of them now. I've been meaning to get a gift for the choir director and these would be perfect."

The priest took out his wallet, and right there in the church, I sold Carlotta's napkins. I wasn't sure how much Carlotta expected for them, but I figured the young priest was more generous than Doña Teresa.

On my way back to the Banyan, I noticed some fancy shops along Duval. If we all worked together, maybe we could persuade some of those shopkeepers to take Carlotta's napkins on consignment. Maybe we could find other ways to work together too and get the Banyan out of hock. The little sprig of hope that had slept inside me for the past few weeks woke up and took notice.

16

H e's here! In the kitchen!" Lynette said, pulling me through the front door.

I still felt hopeful after the priest's promise, but Lynette's worry rushed at me like a cold wind. I tried to tell her my idea, but she didn't give me the chance. Instead, she gripped me by the wrist and pulled me into the dining room.

"There he is," Lynette whispered. We peeked in through the crack of the door like two little kids spying on Santa.

"Some nerve he's got too," Lynette observed. "Sitting at the table like a guest who's been invited to dinner."

I couldn't see a thing on account of the crack being

small and Lynette having grown large enough to fill it ten times over.

"What's he saying?" I whispered.

"I don't know. I didn't even get a good look at him," Lynette whispered back. "I'm supposed to stay on the couch, remember?"

There was some low murmuring and then Carlotta called out, "Irena? Is that you who just came in? Can you come in here please?"

Lynette stepped aside stiffly to let me pass. I could tell by her sagging face that she was hurt that Carlotta had not called her into the kitchen too.

The first thing I noticed was the familiar swirl of overgrown red hair meant to cover an ever-enlarging bald spot.

"Hello, Irena." Will Everett stood up, sucking the coziness right out of Carlotta's kitchen.

"Hello, Will," I said back. My eyes darted to the door leading out into the courtyard. In a minute, Daddy would rush through, ready to pounce. My first instinct was to run, but then I looked at Carlotta's gentle face.

"You don't have to be scared, Irena. I've come by myself," Will said.

Instead of bringing me comfort, Will's words settled down on top of me like a thick fog.

"Sure," I said. "Mama isn't with you." I'd meant to just say the words like an accusation, but my heart failed me and I found myself asking the question again. "Is she, Will?"

Will, his blue eyes just staring, didn't say a word. I'd always loved Will's eyes, blue and clear, unable to lie even if it meant that the lie could save someone.

"I came to tell you about your father," Will said.

A new fear bloomed inside me. The gator powder! Had I used too much? Mad was one thing, but I hadn't ever meant to hurt Daddy, not for good.

"Is Daddy okay?"

"As okay as anybody, I suppose," Will said.

"As good as anybody? What does that mean?" I asked.

Will rubbed his brow like he was working an answer from his brain. Mama had always said Will was smart as a whip, but he needed for people to take time with him to understand him.

"Actually, Irena," Will said. "Your daddy packed up the day after you left. Haven't seen him since. Took my trailer too," Will said, pretending to chuckle. But it came out so halfhearted that it sounded just plain tired. "I guess he figured it was his turn to take something of mine."

"Gone? But where?" I asked, picturing the spot where

the trailer had stood, empty now save for a notch in the sand where the hitch had rested.

"Can't say," Will said.

What felt like hot bile rose up in my throat. Ever since I could remember, home wasn't a city or a house, it was Mama and Daddy. With Mama gone and now Daddy, I felt like a kite whose string has been cut.

"I need a glass of water," I said, turning for the sink. As I stared at the cold water gushing from the faucet, I remembered the day Mama had left for good.

"You'll see! I'll show you!" Mama was screaming at Daddy. I was in my bedroom painting my toenails the way I'd seen them done in my favorite magazine. I was used to my parents fighting by now and only kept half an ear on the ruckus going on out in the living room. But then something Mama yelled caught my attention.

"It's your fault, Dwayne. I fell in love with him, and it's all your fault!"

The sound of a door and Mama screaming, "No, Dwayne! You leave him alone!" had me off my bed and standing in my doorway.

"Mama?" I said, but Mama didn't answer. She was wringing her hands, staring out the screen door. "Where'd Daddy go?" I asked, but still she said nothing.

Of course, looking back on it now, I knew exactly

where Daddy was headed and who Mama was worried about.

A minute later Daddy was back. Two steps ahead of him and looking confused was Will.

"What's all this about, Lil?" Will asked Mama. "Dwayne says you have something to tell me?"

"Go ahead, Lil. Tell Will what you just told me," Daddy said, prodding Mama.

Mama looked so white I thought she might pass out.

"Go ahead, Lil. Tell him!" Daddy yelled. If Daddy had been wrestling a gator at that moment, my prayers would've been for the gator. The light in Mama's eyes was dimming fast.

Will just stood there, gator slime all up and down his pant legs. I wanted to scream at him, to tell him to save Mama, to tell her that he loved her too. But deep down I knew that would only make Mama seem more pathetic, and I didn't want that, no matter how much I wanted her saved.

"Do you see now, Lil?" Daddy said. He was grinning from ear to ear, so self-satisfied, proving to Mama that all of her dreams were just that—dreams.

"Mama?" I said. Mama still stood in the center of the living room, her blue dress hugging the curves of her body, but underneath that dress and that skin, all of the life in Mama had shrunk to the size of a shriveled-up pea.

"Stop it!" I yelled at Daddy for embarrassing her so.

And then I finally turned to Will. "Say something! Make Daddy stop!" I said.

"What do you want me to say?" Will said. The big oaf! He was Mama's Gregory Peck, Rock Hudson, and Steve McQueen all rolled up into one and he didn't have a clue.

Turning off the water without getting a drink, I turned to Will. "How'd you find me?" I asked.

"Some trucker came by one day. He got pretty drunk on moonshine and just started talking. Said he picked up a girl along the trail and brought her down to Key West. Remembered the name of the motel and everything."

"You came after me, but you couldn't go after my mother?" I said. The words came out like poison, like a triple dose of gator powder, but they finally came out and it felt good, like revenge.

"Aw, Irena," Will said, shaking his head. "I wasn't her husband. It was up to your daddy to go after her, not me."

"You knew he wouldn't, Will!" I screamed.

"Irena, *querida*," Carlotta said, stepping forward, but I took a step back. Not even Carlotta could save me from the thick anger that was boiling up around me like hot black tar. I felt myself being pulled under, but I didn't care. Will needed to see what being a coward had done.

"You knew Daddy wouldn't go after her, but why'd you hold me back from going after her, Will? Why'd you do it?" I said. The tears were streaming down my face now. The memory of Will's hands gripping my bare arms and leaving a bruise flashed across my eyes. I'd pinched that bruise blue for six months so I'd not forget what he'd done.

Now it was Will who took a step forward, but I glared at him and he stopped. "There was no stopping your mama from leaving, Irena. I think you know that. Don't you? I just didn't want you to get hurt too."

"No! I don't know that!" I yelled at Will, but I was yelling at Daddy and at myself too. "You could have said the right thing just to get her to stay, but you said nothing! Nothing at all!"

"I couldn't lie," Will explained. "That would've been worse for your mama. And for you."

Worse for me? What was worse than losing my mother?

I wanted to wither away, to go away, but then Carlotta said, *"Querida."* Her voice was barely a whisper, but the

love in it was loud enough even for my broken heart
to hear.

"Why did you come, Will?" I asked.

Will tipped his head bashfully, and for a moment I
saw the friend I'd once had. "I just wanted to make sure
you were okay. And . . ."

"Yes?" I said, hoping that something Will had to say
would make Mama's leaving make sense.

"And that I care about you, and if you ever want to
come back, you have a home with me."

I felt something on my shoulder, firm and sweet. It
was Carlotta's hand.

"Since Mr. Everett found out where you were, he's
been calling almost every day to make sure you're okay,"
Carlotta explained. Her words sounded as dry as the
dust covering Will's boots.

Will cleared his throat. "I promised your father too
that if you came back, I'd take care of you."

"It sounds like your papa loves you, yes?" Carlotta said.

I looked down at the worn linoleum in Carlotta's
kitchen. Daddy, love me? It wasn't something I'd ever
considered. Growing up it had always been Mama and
me on one side of the mountain and Daddy on the

other. Then I thought of what the priest said. Maybe Daddy was doing the best he could. For the first time, I was starting to see the mountain of my life from the other side. Daddy's side.

"If you want, you can come back to the gator farm," Will said. "You were always pretty good with the gators."

Carlotta's hand didn't budge from my shoulder, reminding me of something without saying it outright. The conversation I'd overheard. It hadn't been a banker Carlotta had begged for more time, but Will.

"Thanks for the offer, Will," I said. "But I'm doing pretty good right here."

Will nodded.

After that, Carlotta softened toward Will. "Tonight is Papa's birthday and I've made a special dessert. Would you like to join us?"

Will said he had to get going on account of the gators needed to be fed, but he thanked Carlotta and said, "Wish your papa a happy birthday for me."

On the way out to his truck, Will made me promise to keep his offer in mind.

Before he left, I asked him something else that had been on my mind for quite a while. "What exactly goes into gator powder?"

"Mainly sugar and a little bit of vanilla," Will said.

"Sugar!"

"Why not?" Will said. "The gators love it and the wrestlers think they're putting one over on the gators."

Will and I laughed, and that little bit of laughter helped me remember some of the good times. I was thinking that maybe Will had gotten into the middle of something that had nothing to do with him, a problem Daddy and Mama had that wasn't his fault either.

As Will pulled down Spring Street, I waved and marveled at how I'd never needed the powder at all.

That night, Carlotta set out a dinner fit for a celebration. Chicken and rice, baked yucca stuffed with shredded beef, and pasteles, bits of meat and peppers tucked into plantain leaves.

"These were all of Papa's favorite foods. He would be happy to see us all together," Carlotta said as she dished out the plates.

Lynette and I caught each other's eye. How long would we be able to stay together? When would we all be forced to go our own separate ways? Will's visit did give me a place to go once the Banyan closed for good, but knowing this did nothing to ease the ache in my heart. Looking around the table at Carlotta, Don Antonio, and Lynette, I realized that this was my family now.

After Will had gone, I'd told Lynette my idea for selling Carlotta's napkins.

"It's a nice idea," Lynette said. "But there's the cost of the linen, and embroidery takes time. Time we don't have."

Lynette was right. I'd only been thinking about keeping everyone together, not the time or the money the napkins would cost. Like the gator powder, Carlotta's napkins turned out not to be the magical fix I'd been hoping for.

Surprisingly, when Carlotta filled the mystery guest's plate, Lynette held her tongue. What did the gesture matter anyway? Filling the plate seemed to make Carlotta happy, and why should this be taken away from her too?

After Don Antonio polished off his third helping, Carlotta said, "I hope you've left room for dessert."

Lynette nearly jumped out of her skin. "I'll get it," she offered.

"Are you feeling well enough?" Carlotta asked.

All the rest seemed to have made Lynette restless and she bounded up out of her chair. She took an eternity to come back. Maybe she'd left me to figure things out on my own. Then there she was, carrying a big platter of fried plantains in honey. She just stood there with a big silly grin on her face. Maybe the trouble had finally gotten to her and she had lost her marbles.

"What is it, Lynette?" Carlotta asked.

"I don't know." Lynette giggled nervously.

Then the most amazing thing happened. Lynette found religion. She flung up her arms, the platter of plantains clattering to the floor. "Criminy!" she screamed. "I'm having a baby!"

17

on Antonio and I sat in a corner of the emergency room waiting. To pass the time, we bought hot cups of cocoa from the vending machine that neither of us drank.

When the ambulance had picked Lynette up, I'd overheard one of the EMTs say to the other, "Her water's broke. Can't stop the labor now."

I imagined the baby, as impatient and pinch-faced as Lynette, knocking on Lynette's stomach and demanding to be let out into the world right that instant. If I wasn't so worried, I might've laughed. Don Antonio's jowls drooped lower than usual. I could tell he was worried too.

Carlotta emerged from behind a double door wearing a pair of blue scrubs. Her face looked pink and slick, the way it turned when she'd been standing over a pot of boiling soup for a long time.

Jumping out of my seat, I ran to Carlotta and said, "The baby! How is it? What about Lynette?"

Carlotta slumped down into one of the vinyl chairs. Her curls gathered in sweaty clumps on the back of her neck. "Lynette's fine," she said, smiling. "The baby is small, but she's a fighter just like her mother."

Don Antonio clapped his hands together and I released the breath I'd been holding for the last few hours.

Then I realized Carlotta had said that *she* was a fighter!

"It's a girl!" I said, amazed that Lynette had managed to have her girl after all.

"Lynette wants to see both of you," Carlotta said. "Only one at a time, though. Hospital policy."

Don Antonio went first.

"The doctors say the baby needs time to grow," Carlotta said. "Then we can take her home."

Time? When Vera could come home would there be a home for her to come to?

Don Antonio returned twenty minutes later. "A little treasure! That's what she is," he said.

"Ready?" the same candy striper who had led Don Antonio to see Lynette asked me.

At the end of the hallway, Lynette stood near a large window. She was dressed in a blue terry-cloth robe I'd never seen before. Lynette looked calmer and more beautiful than I'd ever seen her, but the minute she opened her mouth, she was still the same old Lynette.

"Don't let anyone ever tell you that having a baby doesn't hurt," Lynette said instead of a simple hello. "It hurts in a way you never thought hurting could hurt." But then Lynette turned to face the window and said excitedly, "Guess which one she is?"

The choice wasn't a difficult one. In that sea of blue and pink blankets, Vera was the only baby in the nursery with a thick crop of black hair.

"She's beautiful," I told Lynette.

"The doctors say she's doing real good," Lynette said. She bit down on her bottom lip, which was already chapped and now began to bleed.

"She really is beautiful, and she's going to be fine," I reassured Lynette.

Lynette nodded, but for once in her life was speechless.

"Visiting hours are over," a nurse told me. "You can come back to see your sister tomorrow."

"Thanks, Irena," Lynette said, finding her voice again.

"Why don't you sit up front today, Irena?" Carlotta suggested as we all piled into Don Antonio's old Montego for the ride home.

Ordinarily, Carlotta loved sitting up front in the Banana Boat. That was the nickname she'd given to Don Antonio's old car. The jalopy had more rust patches than metal.

"What's the matter, Carlotta?" Don Antonio teased. "Don't you trust my driving?"

This time around Carlotta didn't take the bait. Instead she slid into the backseat, where she remained quiet.

As we chugged through town, I stole looks at Carlotta in the rearview mirror. The smooth serenity I'd seen on her face after Vera's birth seemed to have evaporated, replaced instead by a frown and two sharp lines furrowing her forehead.

When we arrived back at the Banyan Tree, Don Antonio said, "How about a picnic under the banyan to celebrate Vera?"

So as Carlotta and I assembled the Cuban sandwiches—layers of roasted pork, swiss cheese, mustard, and dill pickles on long loaves of crusty bread—Don Antonio searched for the card table.

Carlotta pressed the sandwiches flat on the *plancha*.

"Should I make an extra sandwich for . . ." and I pointed in the direction of the mystery guest's room.

"Not today," Carlotta said.

Carlotta's answer surprised me, but more than that it worried me. I stood by not knowing what to say or do, watching as a dribble of swiss cheese oozed out the sides of the sandwiches that Carlotta was pressing on the *plancha*.

In the yard Don Antonio sat in his green chair waiting for us. He'd taken the folding card table from the shed and arranged all our chairs around it. We ate our sandwiches and drank limeade underneath the cool canopy of the banyan. Freddie joined us, nibbling on the bits of swiss cheese Don Antonio offered him.

The afternoon wore on and the crickets woke and performed a chirpy concert. Their song filled every nook and cranny of the yard and their small loudness reminded me of Vera. She was tiny now, but someday soon she would add her own voice to all the other voices in the world. A world, I was afraid, that would not include Don Antonio's stories about Papa or Carlotta's joy or my love.

After we finished our *cubanos*, we stayed at the table. Don Antonio fell asleep, his breathy snoring gently rippling the napkin tucked into his collar.

Looking at the chairs, I asked Carlotta, "What color should we make Vera's chair?" Even if she would never get a chance to sit in her chair, it didn't seem right for Vera not to have her own.

"Hmm?" Carlotta stared at me blankly. She looked a million miles away. Was Carlotta like Mama? Was she starting to slip away from me too?

"Vera's chair," I said again, trying to hold on. "We need to give her her own chair," I insisted.

"I think it's time I show you something," Carlotta told me.

Carlotta led me to the mystery guest's room, where she pulled a key from her pocket. Watching as Carlotta wiggled the key into the lock, I couldn't believe what she was doing. What if the mystery guest was in there? Or worse. What if he or she found us snooping around where we didn't belong? But Carlotta looked perfectly at ease with the whole notion, as if breaking and entering was something she did every day.

Carlotta flipped on the light switch and the room was bathed in a soft glow. A new white carpet dotted with flecks, like bits of blue and pink confetti, covered the floor. A glossy sheen of pink paint glazed the walls, and a mobile of dancing frogs hung over the most exquisite cradle.

"So that's what I bumped . . ." The words slipped out of my mouth before I could reel them back in.

Carlotta laughed. "I was wondering whose fingerprints were all over my fresh paint."

Heat spread across my cheeks and I tried to explain, but Carlotta just shrugged and said, "What does it matter anymore?"

"It's the most beautiful room I've ever seen," I told Carlotta, trying to lift her out of her glum mood. I ran my hand over the curved rails of the cradle. The wood was as smooth as a baby's cheek.

"It's amazing. But how?" I asked. Then I remembered the day down at the docks, the pallet of wood and the thick roll of bills, a roll as large as Carlotta's heart.

"You did this all for Vera?"

"And for Lynette." Carlotta sighed. "Believe me. It wasn't easy. Lynette was such a nuisance, always breathing down my neck about money. And then you, Irena. You know you make an awful spy."

My face must've fallen a thousand feet because Carlotta laughed and said, "It's okay, Irena. I could tell by the way you were slinking around behind me that you didn't really have your heart in it."

"Oh, Carlotta," I said, giving her a big hug.

"It's okay, *querida*," she told me. Carlotta's face grazed my hair. I could feel warm tears on my scalp.

"What's wrong?" I asked.

"I made up this room for Lynette and the baby because I wanted to give them a good start, but now . . ." Carlotta shook her head. "I'm afraid I've messed up everything." Carlotta looked like a tree hunched over by the weight of her own fruit.

Now I saw. All along, when Carlotta didn't seem to understand or care that the Banyan was in trouble, she'd only been hiding her worry from the rest of us.

"Isn't there anything we can do?" I asked.

"I can't see what else can be done."

Seeing Carlotta so defeated scared me. I was desperate to hang on. But how? All my ideas had been useless. What could a kid like me do that could possibly make a difference?

Pushed over to one side of the room sat an old writing table. Carlotta ran her hand lovingly over the chair. "This room used to be Papa's room," Carlotta explained. "When he wasn't telling Antonio and me stories, he was in here writing or dreaming. It was a special place for him. A home away from home."

That was exactly what the Banyan was for me.

Carlotta opened a desk drawer. It was filled with papers. "See," Carlotta said. "I've even kept some of Papa's stories right here where he left them. Someday, when she is old enough, Vera can read these stories for herself."

What Carlotta was really saying was that Vera would have Papa's stories even when Carlotta and Don Antonio were no longer around to tell them to her. These stories, like the blue room and the Banyan, were pieces of herself that Carlotta wanted to leave behind so that Vera would always remember her.

Thinking about my own mama, about the nights we'd spent in the dark watching movies and talking about our dreams, I said, "Don't worry, Carlotta. Vera will always have you with her no matter what."

Before we left the room, I turned to Carlotta and asked, "If there wasn't a mystery guest, why did you fill an extra plate of food every night?"

"To feed Vera's spirit," Carlotta explained. "Even though she wasn't here in the flesh, her spirit was getting ready to come to us. I just wanted her to know how much she was welcome."

That night, I thought about how people come and go in our lives and how even when they are not with us in the flesh, we could still love them.

❧ 18 ☙

Make sure you pack everything I asked you for," Lynette told me when she called from the hospital that afternoon. Vera was holding her own, and the doctors planned to release Lynette the next day. "And remember my favorite pink shirt," Lynette said.

Stepping into Lynette's room, a great sadness rushed over me. Without Lynette, the room felt empty, like a seashell echoing the ocean even after it's beached. Of course, Lynette in all her loudness would be back tomorrow, but once the Banyan was forced into bankruptcy, then what? Would someone else buy it? Would they even keep it a motel or would they just knock the whole place down to make room for condominiums?

Lynette's broken heart charm still hung from her lamp. The salt air had pitted the metal. Taking it in my hand, I pressed the charm to my mouth, blew on it, then rubbed the charm on my shirt until it shined.

Into one of Carlotta's mesh market bags, I placed two pairs of clean underwear, a bra, Lynette's toothbrush, and the sunflower dress she had, up until today, always complained was too colorful for her. I topped the pile of things with the nubby bunny.

In case Lynette changed her mind about the dress, I found a pair of shorts and a shirt to add to the bag. When I folded the shirt, something poked out of the front pocket. It was the pamphlet from the Hemingway house. The one the man had given to us when we'd paid our admission.

How hopeful I'd felt that day. I'd truly believed that if only I tried hard enough I would find a way to save the Banyan.

Looking at the pamphlet now, I read:

Ernest Hemingway was born on July 21, 1899. Besides being a great writer, he was a wish fulfiller who knew how to make his dreams come true. Hemingway settled in Key West and wrote many of his famous books here. Hemingway loved Key West and the people of Key West loved him too. In fact, the people called him Papa.

On the flip side of the pamphlet was a picture of Hemingway's house. Sitting on the front porch of the house was the burly, bearded man everyone called Papa. Not believing my eyes, I read through the rest of the pamphlet.

Ernest Hemingway lived in Key West from 1929 to 1940. His wife's name was Pauline, and the couple had two sons named Patrick and Gregory.

It didn't make sense!

I rushed to Carlotta's room, but she wasn't there. Fumbling for my key ring, I let myself in. I grabbed up the photo of Carlotta and her papa. The man pictured on the pamphlet was one and the same. What was going on?

"Is it true?" I said, running into the kitchen.

Carlotta was busy in the kitchen putting cookies in a tin to take to the nurses and doctors at the hospital. "What do you have there?" Carlotta said, looking at the pamphlet I was shoving at her.

"Ah! Papa," Carlotta said.

"*This* is your father? *This* is the papa you and Don Antonio are always talking about?"

"No, Irena. Papa wasn't my real father," Carlotta said.

I was really confused now.

"Let me explain, Irena," Carlotta said. "When my mother and my father first came to Key West, they dreamed of opening up a motel. In those days, not many tourists came to Key West, but they worked very hard and they were able to buy the Banyan. Things were going well for a few years, but when I was about three years old, my father died." Carlotta closed the lid on the cookie tin.

"My uncles tried to help my mother. They gave her money, but it was never enough to keep the Banyan going. Then Papa showed up one day and asked Mama if he could rent a room from her. Well, he gave her enough money and told some of his famous friends about the place, so Mama was able to keep the Banyan going."

Carlotta sat down. Her shoulders sagged slightly, and she looked more tired than I'd ever seen her. "Don Antonio and I were young when our own father died," Carlotta said. "I guess Papa Hemingway was the closest we ever came to having a father. Love doesn't always come from the places you expect, Irena. But when it comes, it's important to embrace it."

Carlotta was right, and all I could do was hug her.

"One more question," I said.

"What is it, *querida*?"

"Why would Ernest Hemingway stay here when he had his own house in Key West?" I asked.

Carlotta smiled. "Well, I guess everyone needs to run away from home from time to time."

As we made our way down the hospital corridor toward the nursery, I suddenly remembered something. "Carlotta! Those papers in Vera's room, the ones you showed me yesterday. Do those belong to Ernest Hemingway?"

"Those scribbles? Yes. I suspect they are his. I haven't touched that old desk in years," Carlotta said.

"Scribbles!" I laughed so loud that a nurse shhhed me to keep my voice down.

But nothing could keep my hope quiet anymore because I knew that Papa was about to save the Banyan again.

Epilogue

The flan jiggled as I set it down next to the other desserts. The card table was too small so Don Antonio had bought a larger one, and he'd set it up in the backyard. Besides flan, Carlotta and I had prepared *arroz con leche, casadielles,* and *bizcocho amarillo.*

"Is everything ready for the celebration?" Don Antonio asked, surveying the table. He was wearing his good jacket, the one with the brass buttons. He looked like a ship's captain ready to set sail on an exciting adventure.

"Yes, Don Antonio. Everything is ready," I said, but my smile stretched uncomfortably across my lips.

That morning, as I stirred the rice and milk together

for the *arroz con leche,* Lynette came into the kitchen. In her hand she held an envelope.

"From Miami," Lynette said. In the year that had passed since Vera's birth, Lynette and I had grown closer, but she'd always stay a snoop.

"Thanks," I said. My heart fell at the sight of my father's chicken-scratch handwriting.

"Are you going to read it?" Lynette asked.

Carlotta was in the dining room, but at the sound of her cheerful humming, I said, "No. Not now."

Carlotta came out to see how everything was coming along for the celebration. "Are you okay, *querida*?" she asked.

"Just tired," I lied.

"And no wonder. You have been working nonstop. Well, today all of your hard work will pay off," Carlotta said and she gave me a big hug. For as long as I lived I would never ever get tired of Carlotta's hugs.

Over the rim of the table, I spied a little hand, pudgy and white, reaching up to swipe a cookie.

"No, no, Vera," I said. "Not before dinner." I scooped up the one-year-old into my arms. Just like her mother, Vera didn't like the word *no.* She squeezed up her face and pouted her lips into the shape of a small pink rosette. But Vera's pout was no match for my tickles.

"Who's my girl?" I said, pressing my lips on the back of her neck and blowing ticklish air. Vera's lips blossomed into a full smile. "How about a story?" I suggested.

I carried Vera to the spot under the banyan where Don Antonio sat, entertaining the tourists who had gathered with stories about Papa Hemingway.

"Let me tell you about the time, when I was a boy, that Papa played a prank on me," Don Antonio began.

Vera settled onto Don Antonio's knee and he hugged her close, never skipping a beat in his story. I didn't sit. By now, I knew all of Papa's stories by heart. Instead I returned to the table, pretending to make last-minute arrangements to the dessert buffet.

The pamphlet Lynette and I had made up told what would come next. After Don Antonio's stories, the tourists could take a tour around the motel and see Papa's manuscripts, which were now carefully preserved under glass. They would also be able to enjoy some of Carlotta's fabulous desserts. The pamphlet had other important information about the Banyan Tree too, like its history and room rates.

I put my hand in my pocket, feeling for Daddy's letter, but then thought better of it. No. Not now or today, but maybe tomorrow, I decided. I had promised myself that, no matter what, today would be perfect.

Before the crowd started milling around, I took in the scene. Don Antonio meowed and the crowd of tourists roared with laughter. Vera scooted off Don Antonio's knee and a loud clatter of pots and pans chimed out from the kitchen window. Inside Carlotta was cooking and Lynette was getting ready to give tours. The tourists leaned back on the new white seats we'd bought for the celebration. But when the day was over, the first thing I planned to do was go to the shed and replace the white chairs with our own colorful ones.